T0161169

PIEDMONT
PHANTOMS

Also by Daniel W. Barefoot

Haunted North Carolina: Seaside Spectres

Haunted North Carolina: Haints of the Hills

Touring the Backroads of North Carolina's Upper Coast

Touring the Backroads of North Carolina's Lower Coast

Touring North Carolina's Revolutionary War Sites

Touring South Carolina's Revolutionary War Sites

General Robert F. Hoke: Lee's Modest Warrior

PIEDMONT PHANTOMS

DANIEL W. BAREFOOT

BLAIR

DURHAM, NORTH CAROLINA

Blair is an imprint of Carolina Wren Press.

The mission of Blair/Carolina Wren Press is to seek out, nurture,
and promote literary work by new and underrepresented writers.

This book was supported by the Durham Arts Council's Annual Arts Fund and the
N.C. Arts Council, a division of the Department of Natural & Cultural Resources.

ISBN paperback 9781949467147
ISBN ebook 9781949467222
Library of Congress Control Number: 2019941191

To Kay and Kris,
who have filled my life and our home
in the Piedmont with boundless love
and happiness

Contents

Foreword   ix
Preface   xii
Acknowledgments   xvi

Alamance County: Haunted by the Past   3
Anson County: The Cave at Indian Rock   7
Cabarrus County: A Man's Treasure, a Woman's Grave   10
Caswell County: In Search of Justice   14
Chatham County: A Promise Kept   19
Cumberland County: "Free! Oh, Free!"   23
Davidson County: Guardians of the King's Treasure   26
Davie County: Justice from beyond the Grave   32
Durham County: All for the Love of Gold   37
Forsyth County: Moravian Stars   42
Franklin County: Lady in Blue   46
Gaston County: The Drip, Drip, Drip of Dark Blue Blood   50
Granville County: The Dark Side of Divination   56
Guilford County: Theatrical Haunt   61
Harnett County: Ghosts with a Scottish Accent   66
Hoke County: The Night They Came from the Skies   71
Iredell County: A Bridge to the Supernatural   75
Johnston County: The Spirit(ed) Battle Rages On   78
Lee County: The Sins of the Father   87
Lincoln County: Malvina of Woodside   90

Mecklenburg County: Haunted Chambers 94
Montgomery County: The Witch of Tuckertown 99
Moore County: For Whom Doth the Bell Toll? 102
Nash County: A Mystery within a Mystery 107
Orange County: The Haunting of Seven Hearths 111
Person County: When Fear Was Real 115
Randolph County: The Hunter at the Zoo 120
Richmond County: The Warlock by the River 124
Robeson County: Ghostly Legacy of the Swamp Fox 129
Rockingham County: The Incident at Settle's Bridge 134
Rowan County: The Murderer Who Refused to Die 137
Scotland County: Booger Hill 141
Stanly County: A Prescription for Terror 144
Stokes County: The Spirit of Independence 151
Union County: Phantom Patriots 155
Vance County: Doppelgänger! 158
Wake County: Capitol Haunts 164
Warren County: The Devil's Footprint 171
Wilson County: The Roots of
   America's Most Famous Haunting 174
Yadkin County: Haunts of a Tragic Past 182

Foreword

"I love North Carolina."

A simple statement—and one Dan Barefoot didn't have to tell me. I could tell it myself while propped in my favorite chair, *Haints of the Hills* in my hand, *Piedmont Phantoms* and *Seaside Spectres* on the table beside me. Ghost stories, sure, but the pages of all three are imbued with Dan's love of the state. His fascination with it, too. And that's a powerful combination: love and fascination. So powerful, in fact, I'm afraid I've dog-eared my three volumes and bent the corners of several pages—I'm not one for bookmarks anyway. It's just that I've read and reread his accounts, and no, the supernatural tales haven't kept me up at night, but they have reminded me why I, too, love the state. For it is rich with history, and history is also imbued on the pages of Dan's books, on just about each and every page, which lends credibility to his ghostly stories. And how about that for a combination? Credibility and ghosts?

"Do you believe in them?" I ask Dan—I suppose I'm putting him on the spot. "Ghosts?"

"Well . . ." he begins.

I'm not sure how I'd answer, either. I've told dozens of ghost stories myself, not in print but on TV, and I've looked into the eyes of people who've told me of their encounters with the inexplicable. And not just run-of-the-mill inexplicable, not just weird head-scratchers, but experiences far more bizarre and otherworldly. And yet the people I interviewed seemed so genuine and down-to-earth; many were business professionals with nothing to gain by spinning some far-out, cockamamie story.

"I'm not sure about ghosts," Dan finally admits, and I can't say I blame him. I'd probably respond the same way—I'm a reporter, after all; for fairness sake, it's always best to strike a middle-of-the road position. But Dan doesn't leave it at "not sure." He once again dives into the history of the state, and I nod in agreement. His tales are grounded in history, and there's no getting around historical documentation. Thanks, Dan; reporters love hard facts. With history as foundation, the stories in his books ring . . . true? Well . . . maybe . . . could be . . . not sure. But aren't they intriguing to consider?

Intriguing, in part, because these are little-known ghost stories, and everybody likes to learn something new—especially reporters. "I didn't want to do stories that were beaten to death," Dan tells me, and I admire his choice of words when talking about the ghoulish: *beaten to death.*

Mr. Barefoot has pricked my curiosity. *How did Dan find these hidden stories?* I wonder. *How did he unearth them?* I can only imagine. It must have been like searching for unmarked graves without a flashlight and exhuming the past without a shovel. But, no, turns out it's nothing that shadowy—or sweaty. Dan tells me he visited libraries, and when their research was lacking, he did his own digging, talked to people, visited places, read accounts. "Just had to do the hard work," he says. Although he was used to that—the hard work, that is.

In 2001, Dan was proudly serving in the NC General Assembly when lawmakers considered eliminating North Carolina history for eighth-grade students in public schools—it was taught only in fourth and eighth grades anyway, and this was going to slash North Carolina history in half. Representative Dan must have felt like a scheming demon had suddenly cast a wicked spell. How evil! The

Acknowledgments

Writing a three-volume work with subject matter from each of the one hundred counties of North Carolina has given me a much deeper appreciation for the vastness of the state. To complete a project of this size and scope, I needed the assistance and kindly offices of innumerable people and many institutions. To all of them, I am truly grateful. There are, however, individuals who deserve special mention for their efforts on my behalf.

Extensive research was essential for the successful completion of this project. Librarians and their assistants at numerous county and municipal libraries throughout the state helped in that task by searching for materials, offering advice, and extending other courtesies to me. Pat Harden of the Norris Public Library in Rutherfordton; Chris Bates, the curator of the Carolina Room at the Public Library of Charlotte-Mecklenburg County; and Fred Turner of the Olivia Raney Local History Library in Raleigh were particularly helpful. At the reference section in the State Library of North Carolina and in the search room of the North Carolina State Archives, I always received prompt and courteous attention and assistance. At the University of North Carolina at Chapel Hill, Bob Anthony and his staff at the North

only way to break such a curse was to roll up the sleeves, dig down, author a bill. The legislation he drafted mandated that North Carolina history stay put in eighth grade. In the end, he stared the demon down, and his bill became law. (Dan, next time I see a ghost I'm calling you).

"I love North Carolina, and I did not want to leave any part of North Carolina out," he says, referring to his three volumes, in which all one hundred counties are represented, a ghost story from each one. And history in each, too. "You can go to all one hundred counties and find something special," he says. "From Dare County to the Tennessee line. I enjoy every part of it because of its history."

I know what he means. I've traveled to all one hundred counties myself, and I'm always amazed at what I find: the memorable people, awe-inspiring sights, and great historical nuggets. There's a pleasant surprise around every bend—well, except maybe when an apparition appears out of nowhere.

"I love the state because of its history," Dan says again, and he seems rather passionate, and I like that—the passion. And yet, he pauses a moment, and I sense he's gathering himself before ending the interview with a final flourish—I bet he was a great delegate and am sure he's still a stellar lawyer; I'd like to see him in a courtroom sometime.

He clears his throat, and the end is short and sweet and to the point—with just enough drama, a bit of a cliffhanger.

"North Carolina . . ." he says. "It is history steeped in tradition. And mystery."

Scott Mason

Scott Mason is the star and host of the Tar Heel Traveler feature series and specials for WRAL-TV in Raleigh, NC and author of five books about his Tar Heel Traveler adventures across the state.

Preface

From ghoulies and ghosties and long-leggety beasties
And things that go bump in the night,
Good Lord, deliver us.

Scottish prayer

The Piedmont of North Carolina is a very special place for me: I was born here; I was educated here; I met my wife here; I was married here; our daughter was born here; and I have lived my entire life here. And the Piedmont's fascinating folklore and supernatural history have intrigued me for as long as I can remember.

As a child growing up in North Carolina in the 1950s and 1960s, I delighted in watching Rod Serling's *The Twilight Zone* television series and the great science-fiction films of that period. At the same time, I read with great interest the classic ghost stories of North Carolina, as documented by John Harden in *The Devil's Tramping Ground* (1949) and *Tar Heel Ghosts* (1954) and by Nancy Roberts in *An Illustrated Guide to Ghosts & Other Mysterious Occurrences in the Old North State* (1959) and *Ghosts of the Carolinas* (1962).

Meanwhile, I was developing an abiding interest in the magnificent history of North Carolina. The history of the state—indeed, the history of British America—began on the soil of North Carolina with Sir Walter Raleigh's colonization attempts, which resulted in the Lost Colony of Roanoke in the 1580s. Ironically, our history as Tar Heels began with a haunting mystery that remains unresolved to this day.

When the European traditions of ghosts, witches, demons, and the like were brought to America, they landed on the shores of North Carolina. And it was on our soil that settlers documented some of the first encounters with the supernatural in America. But long before the arrival of European settlers, North Carolina was the domain of various Indian peoples. Theirs is a history replete with tales of the supernatural.

Because North Carolina has been a significant part of the American experience from the very beginning, it has emerged as one of the most historic places in the United States. And where there is history, ghosts and other elements of the supernatural can usually be found. As a longtime student of the Old North State, I can assure readers that North Carolina has a haunted heritage, one rich in the supernatural.

This book and its companion volumes offer a view of that ghostly history in a format never before presented. Here, for the first time, readers are offered a supernatural tale from each of the state's one hundred counties. But the *North Carolina's Haunted Hundred* series is not simply a collection of Tar Heel ghost stories from every county in the state. Rather, it is a sampler of the diverse supernatural history of North Carolina. The three volumes contain accounts of ghosts and apparitions (human, animal, and inanimate), witches, strange creatures, demons, spook lights, haunting mysteries, unidentified flying objects, unexplained phenomena, and more.

Instead of retelling the timeless ghost stories so well

chronicled by Harden, Roberts, Fred T. Morgan, F. Roy Johnson, Judge Charles Harry Whedbee, and others, I have chosen to present many tales that have never been widely circulated in print. I include a few of the familiar tales of our ghostly lore in the mix, but with new information or a new twist.

Do you believe in ghosts and creatures of the night? Whether your answer is yes or no, almost everyone enjoys a ghost story or an inexplicable tale of the unusual. And when that narrative has as its basis real people, actual places, and recorded events, it becomes more enjoyable because it hints at credibility and believability.

All of the stories set forth in this three-volume series are based in fact. But over the years, these tales have been told and retold, and the details have in some cases become blurred. As with all folklore, whether you choose to believe any or all of the accounts in these pages is entirely up to you. A caveat that Mark Twain once offered his readers holds true here: "I will set down a tale. . . . It may be only a legend, a tradition. It may have happened, it may not have happened. But it could have happened."

Should you develop a desire to visit some of the haunted places detailed in this series, be mindful that most are located on private property. Be sure to obtain permission from the owner before attempting to go upon any site.

Sprawling between the expansive coastal plain and the lofty peaks of the mountains is the populous North Carolina Piedmont. The majority of the state's eight million-plus citizens call this region home. Lurking among this crowd of humanity is a sizable population of spirits and unknown entities that I have chosen to refer to collectively as *Piedmont Phantoms*. Their haunted realm now awaits you.

Carolina Collection and the staff at the Southern Historical Collection rendered the same outstanding assistance as they did on my prior books. At other academic libraries in the state, including those at Duke University, East Carolina University, and Appalachian State University, the special-collections personnel helped to point me in the right direction in my quest for information.

This project represents the fifth time around for me in working with Carolyn Sakowski and the excellent staff at John F. Blair, Publisher. Carolyn saw the merit in my proposal from the outset, and she was instrumental in its evolution into a three-book set. As in each of my past efforts, Steve Kirk has gone beyond the call of duty to provide his expertise as my editor. His patience, good and timely advice, keen insight, and knowledge of many subjects are deeply appreciated, and his hard work has added immeasurably to the quality of this book. Debbie Hampton, Anne Waters, Ed Southern, and all of the others at Blair are a pleasure to work with in production, publicity, and marketing.

When I issued a request for "good" ghost stories, my colleagues in the North Carolina General Assembly came to the aid of the person they refer to as their "resident historian." Special assistance was provided by Representative Bill Hurley of Fayetteville, Representative Phil Haire of Sylva, Representative Wayne Goodwin of Hamlet, and Representative Leslie Cox of Sanford.

Friends from far and wide provided support for my efforts. At the University of North Carolina at Wilmington, my friend and fellow author Dr. Chris Fonvielle offered advice and encouragement. In my hometown of Lincolnton, my friends often greeted me with a common question: "What are you writing now, Dan?" When I responded with details about *North Carolina's Haunted Hundred*, they were universally enthusiastic about the series. My crosstown friend, George Fawcett, considered by many to be the foremost authority on unidentified flying objects in North Carolina, welcomed the opportunity to provide from his vast files materials on a credible UFO landing on Tar Heel soil. Darrell Harkey, the Lincoln County historical coordinator, provided words of encouragement and friendship when they were needed most.

For its unending assistance, support, and love, I owe my family an enormous debt of gratitude I can never repay. Because of my family roots, I hold a close kinship with each of the three geographic regions in the *Haunted Hundred* set. In the 1920s, my paternal grandparents left their home in Columbus County on the coast to settle in Gaston County. About the same time, my maternal grandparents left their home in western North Carolina to put down roots in Gaston. In that Piedmont county, east thus met west, and my parents married and reared a son there.

My late father introduced me to the intriguing world of ghosts and the supernatural by taking me to those now-campy horror films of the late fifties and early sixties. My mother taught me the love of reading and writing at an early age. Both parents instilled in me a love of my native state.

My sister remains an ardent supporter of my career as a writer and historian.

My daughter, Kristie, has literally grown up while I have written eight books over the past seven years. With forbearance and love, she has endured the travels and travails of a father who has attempted to balance a career in law, politics, and history with a normal family life. Now a junior at the University of North Carolina at Chapel Hill, she has somehow found time in her extremely busy schedule to type portions of my handwritten manuscripts.

No one deserves more praise and credit for this book and all my others than my wife and best friend, Kay. It was Kay who encouraged me to combine my interests in North Carolina history and the supernatural heritage of our state to produce this book and its companion volumes. As with my previous books, Kay has meticulously read and reread every word and has acted as my sounding board for sentence structure and vocabulary. But more than that, her smiling face, her praise for me even when it's not merited, her willingness to support my every endeavor and to proudly stand beside me, her genuine kindness and unique grace, and her boundless love and constant companionship for more than twenty-seven years have blessed my life with a measure of happiness that few men ever have the good fortune to enjoy.

PIEDMONT
PHANTOMS

Haunted by the Past

Ghosts must be all over the country, as thick as the sands of the sea.

Henrik Ibsen

From the Atlantic coast to the Blue Ridge Mountains, countless ghosts haunt the Tar Heel landscape. Many of these spectres are believed to be the spirits of persons who died tragic, violent deaths as a result of crime, accident, or suicide. Though North Carolina ghosts are found along highways and railroads, on bridges, in cemeteries, and at schools and businesses, their most frequent haunt is the home. Indeed, haunted houses are synonymous with ghosts.

Traditionally, haunted houses have been depicted as dark, forbidding, dilapidated structures devoid of human occupancy for years. But North Carolina boasts numerous well-maintained, historic residences that are inhabited by both living people and ghosts. One such haunted house is in the small community of Alamance in the county of the same name. Located on Friendship Church Road near the E. M. Holt School, the expansive, three-story nineteenth-century house is picturesquely situated on a high knoll above the road. To protect the privacy of the current and past owners, their names and the name of the house have been changed for the purposes of this story. Nonetheless, the events chronicled herein are true.

For nearly seventy-five years, strange phenomena have been witnessed in the Carter House–phantom footsteps, mysterious bloodstains, chilling apparitions. Within its walls, numerous hair-raising incidents have taken place.

Things started during the first half of the twentieth century, when the house was owned by Evan Cane, a member of one of the most respected families in the county. For a number of reasons that will be revealed as this story unfolds, Cane was considered the black sheep of the family. Local gossip was that he operated a moonshine still along the banks of the creek in back of the property.

When the authorities were tipped off about the still, they began to look for its owner. Before Evan Cane could be questioned, he decided to end his life. While sitting at the kitchen table one day, the troubled man put a loaded pistol to his head and pulled the trigger. That evening, Cane's son came home from his job to find his father sitting in a chair. When he patted his father on the shoulder, the lifeless corpse fell to the floor, and blood poured out of his wound on to the oak boards. Friends speculated that Evan Cane took his life in order to avoid a prison sentence and to spare his family embarrassment and shame.

Following his death, the house passed from the ownership of the Cane family. Almost immediately after they moved in, the new owners began to hear inexplicable sounds in various parts of the residence. The stately structure soon acquired a reputation as a haunted house. All of the subsequent owners reported supernatural occurrences.

One recent set of owners, the Dick Carter family, has documented a number of spooky incidents. Not long after Mr. and Mrs. Carter took up residence in the rambling dwelling, they were intrigued that the kitchen door leading to the back porch would not stay closed. Each time the family sat down for a meal, the closed door would mysteriously spring open. It was as if an unseen entity were making an entrance.

There was something else about the kitchen that the Carters quickly learned: a dark stain was prominent at the very spot where Evan Cane had killed himself many years before. Although Mrs. Carter could not tell whether the mysterious stain was blood, paint, or some other substance, she discovered that it could not be permanently removed, despite her repeated efforts. When the Carters renovated the house, they decided to cover the sinister spot with tile.

But there have been other bizarre happenings that the owners were unable to hide. Strange footsteps in the second- and third-floor bedrooms have been heard by occupants of the first-floor den when there was no other person in the house. At other times, family members retiring to their second-floor chambers have heard the ominous sounds of someone or something pacing very lightly without shoes on the third floor. On occasion, family members have been startled from a deep sleep by footsteps in the kitchen. Brave souls have left the safety and comfort of their beds to search for the source of the noise, but nothing has ever been found. For lack of a better explanation, the Carters believe that it could be the spirit of Evan Cane tracing his final steps before the suicide.

Although Mr. and Mrs. Carter have never seen a ghost in the house, a former resident told them of a terrifying apparition. Mrs. Louise Herbert related the incident when she stopped by her old home to admire the renovations being made to it. When the Carters mentioned their unnerving experiences, Mrs. Herbert acknowledged that the house might be haunted by a second ghost. On one occasion, when Mrs. Herbert's infant granddaughter and the child's mother spent the night at the house, the little girl began crying in the wee hours of the morning. After a considerable time, the wailing did not subside, so Mrs. Herbert arose from bed, turned on the light in the hall, and quietly entered the adjacent bedroom, where she supposed her daughter-in-law was still asleep. To her surprise, the child's mother was lying in her bed wide awake. Mrs. Herbert asked why she had not attended to the needs of the baby. The young woman had a look of terror in her eyes. Her lips quivering with every word, she stammered, "There was a woman with long blond hair standing over there looking at me. When you turned the light on, she vanished."

After learning of this frightening incident, Mrs. Carter made further inquiries into the history of the house and its former occupants. From that investigation came information that Evan Cane had been having an affair with a local trollop at the time he took his life. The woman lived nearby with her illegitimate son. As Mrs. Carter delved further into the mystery, she learned that Evan Cane was speculated to have killed himself as a result of the mistaken impression that his mistress was carrying his child. Could it be that the ghost of this loose woman has taken residence here with the ghost of her lover?

Fortunately, no one has been physically harmed by the weird happenings in the Carter House. Apparently, the resident spirits have no malevolent intent. But the disconcerting sights and sounds will no doubt continue to scare residents and guests.

There is a moral to this story. Should you be in the market to purchase a house, particularly an old one, be sure to check into its history. Otherwise, you may be forced to share space with the ghostly inhabitants of one of the many haunted houses found throughout North Carolina.

The Cave at Indian Rock

If the devil doesn't exist, but man has created him, he has created him in his own image and likeness.

Fyodor Dostoevsky

Geographers and historians have often referred to Bladen County as the "Mother of Counties" in North Carolina, since so many of the state's one hundred counties were created from land that once fell within Bladen's boundaries. Perhaps a more appropriate nickname would be "Grandmother of Counties," for it was Bladen's first child, Anson County, that gave birth to all of the counties in the western half of the state. Established in 1750 as the fifteenth county in the colony, Anson once stretched westward from Bladen to the Mississippi River and included all of what is now the state of Tennessee. Now greatly reduced in size, the modern county covers 536 square miles.

Historians believe that the first white settler put down roots in the area now encompassed by Anson in 1740. Prior to that time, this land was the domain of the Catawba Indians. And so, in this ancient county, it is fitting that Anson's oldest haunted spot should be associated with its Indian residents of long ago.

Approximately three and a half miles northeast of the county seat of Wadesboro, NC 742 crosses Gould's Fork Creek. Located not far from the highway bridge in an almost inaccessible location is a small, spooky cave that has been the site of strange happenings and bizarre tales since the arrival of Anson's first permanent settlers.

Catawba hunting parties in search of shelter are said to have carved the cavern out of solid rock. In its dark, damp, creepy interior is a single room. It measures roughly eight by ten feet and has enough clearance for a man of average height to walk in relative comfort. Strange markings—not the usual graffiti—are on the walls. Odd-shaped holes in the cavern are said to have held the peace pipes of the Indians.

While camping here, the Catawbas reportedly buried gold on the surrounding property. As a result, the adjacent landscape is pockmarked with many holes—evidence of the treasure hunting that has gone on here. As far as anyone knows, none of the precious metal hidden by the Indians has ever been found. And for good reason. Few people who have mustered the courage to venture to this ominous place have lingered long, for phantom voices emanate from the vicinity of the cave. The strange voices are said to belong to Indian spirits who gather at the site to discuss their gold.

A man whose house stood nearby refused to rebuild his dwelling in the mid-1950s after the original structure burned. Instead, he chose to live elsewhere because of the frightening voices coming from the Indian Rock, as the cave is known locally.

There is more to the legend. After the Catawbas were forced to abandon the cave following the influx of white settlers, the darkest, most menacing of all supernatural forces took up residence at the Indian Rock. The devil himself slept in the cave and used a nearby natural stone floor as his racetrack. Close by is an enormous, flat rock set flush with the ground. Much in the tradition of the more famous Devil's Tramping Ground in Chatham County, items placed on the stone bed during daylight hours mysteriously vanish when darkness engulfs this desolate place. Area residents claim that Satan removes the objects when he uses his racetrack under cover of night.

So remote and so hidden are the cave and the racetrack that they are almost impossible to find. Maybe that is as it should be. Most folks in Anson County agree that it is best to leave both the ghosts of the Catawbas, who guard hidden gold, and the devil, who amuses himself at his stone race course, to their supernatural devices at this place called Indian Rock.

A Man's Treasure, A Woman's Grave

Evil flourishes far more in the shadows than in the light of day.

Jawaharlal Nehru

Throughout recorded history, gold has consistently remained one of the most valuable commodities in the world. Because of its enduring value, the precious metal has been associated with crime, mystery, intrigue, and greed down through the ages. It is not surprising, then, that at the beginning of the nineteenth century, in the wake of the opening of the first gold mine in North Carolina, one of its shafts was the setting of a mysterious crime. Even today, the cries of the ghost of the unfortunate murder victim can be heard and its presence felt in the famous Reed Gold Mine.

Cabarrus County emerged as the site of the first gold rush in the United States not long after twelve-year-old Conrad Reed pulled a seventeen-pound nugget from Meadow Creek on his father's farm on a Sunday morning in 1799. When the lad displayed his find to his parents, they didn't know what it was. For a time, Conrad's father, John Reed, used it for a doorstop. It was in 1802 that he finally learned it was gold. John Reed sold the entire piece in Fayetteville for what he termed "a big price"—three dollars and fifty cents.

When he returned home, John was delighted to find numerous pieces of gold—some even larger than the first chunk—scattered in the creek. Cognizant that his farm was literally resting atop a gold mine, the former Hessian soldier of the American Revolution associated himself with several local businessmen. Together, they opened the mine that continues to bear Reed's name. From the time the Reed Gold Mine commenced operation until the California gold rush of the mid-nineteenth century, Cabarrus County and the surrounding area led the nation in gold production.

Extensive manpower was required to bring forth the copious quantities of gold from the mine on the Reed farm. Every day, large numbers of men descended the deep, dark shafts to harvest the treasure. In order to ensure that the laborers did not steal any of the precious metal, mine bosses monitored activities below the surface. One such overseer at the Reed Gold Mine was a coarse, hard-drinking man known to the miners and most other people in the community simply as "Boss."

Despite his callous nature, Boss somehow convinced a lovely blond Englishwoman to marry him. From the beginning, however, the marriage was beset with problems. Boss did little to endear himself to his strikingly beautiful bride. She quickly soured on the relationship and developed a strong desire to return to England.

One night, after hours of ceaseless squabbling, Boss agreed to allow his wife to make the transatlantic voyage to visit her family and friends. The greatly relieved woman promptly packed her belongings into trunks and made preparations for the trip, which would take her to Charlotte by horse and buggy, to New York City by train, and then to England by ship. The joyous news was sent ahead to her family across the sea.

Early one Tuesday morning, after his wife exchanged fare-wells with her friends, Boss took the reins of the fully loaded horse-drawn buggy. Off they went on the eight-hour journey to Charlotte. No one ever again saw the woman alive.

Boss reported for work at the "lower hill" at the regular time on Wednesday morning. Weeks passed without incident, until his wife's family reported that their loved one had not arrived as expected. Boss was somewhat defensive about the matter. He insisted that he had put his wife on the train in Charlotte.

A subsequent investigation yielded no leads to the disappear-ance. It was as if the woman had vanished from the face of the earth. Given Boss's reputation as a ruffian, gossip spread through-out the mining community that he had done away with his wife.

One morning, a miner informed Boss that he had detected a strong, foul smell at the entrance to an unworked tunnel. Ac-companied by three workers, Boss made his way to the site and was quick to volunteer to lead the way into the shaft to de-termine the source of the odor. Several other men, holding candles high to provide illumination, followed their foreman at a distance.

As the little expedition made its way into the bowels of the earth, the tunnel narrowed to the point that there was room for only one person. Boss forged onward while the others remained behind, holding their candles in such a way as to provide light for him. From their vantage point, they could see only the shadow of Boss dragging something deeper into the shaft. Finally, when he was near the end of the tunnel, Boss pulled out a stick of dynamite, lit it, and ordered everyone to run for the entrance.

After the explosion, Boss informed the miners that the ter-rible odor had come from a dead animal, perhaps a stray pack horse. He explained that, to remedy the situation, he had pulled the carcass to where the blast would cover the decaying body. Boss was taken at his word, and no one gave any further thought to the incident.

As the years passed, the mysterious disappearance of the Englishwoman remained unsolved. Then, one day, a group of mine explorers worked their way to the end of the shaft that Boss had dynamited. There, they found a variety of intriguing items: a woman's slipper, a plait of blond hair, a flat gold nugget, and a locket. Eyewitnesses said that the nugget was in the shape of the profile of a woman with long, golden hair. Old-timers in the community claimed that the profile was the likeness of Boss's wife. Furthermore, they confirmed that the locket, the slipper, and the hair belonged to the missing woman. But no one was ever able to conclusively prove that Boss had killed his wife and disposed of her body in the Reed Gold Mine.

Soon after the items were discovered, weird, frightening cries were heard in the shaft. Miners suddenly began to experience the feeling that an invisible presence was moving about them in the tunnel where they were working.

Today, Reed Gold Mine State Historic Site, located approximately twenty-eight miles north of Charlotte, preserves the place where John Reed and North Carolina struck it rich in 1802. If you are brave enough to venture into the haunted shaft on a tour, listen carefully for the ghostly screams of a murdered bride. And don't be shocked if you feel a sudden swish of air, as if someone has just rushed past you. Remember, it's only the ghost of a beautiful, homesick woman who is still trying to make her way to her beloved England.

In Search of Justice

*Vex not his ghost: O! Let him pass; he hates him
That would upon the rack of this tough world
Stretch him out longer.*

William Shakespeare

Ghosts are often associated with people who
have met violent deaths either as a result of crimes or accidents.
And so it is with the ghost that haunts the courthouse in Caswell
County. Since State Senator John Walker Stephens was murdered
in 1870 in a room below the main courtroom, his ghost has inhabited the halls of justice.

Located in the heart of Yanceyville, the Caswell County
Courthouse was erected in 1861. It survives today as a magnificent piece of nineteenth-century architecture. Fire caused serious damage to the structure in 1953, but an extensive restora-
tion project in 1968 resulted in its inclusion on the National
Register of Historic Places six years later.

A state historical marker on the street adjacent to the courthouse calls attention to the murder of John Walker Stephens, which occurred in the building a decade after it was constructed. Though he was elected to the state legislature, Stephens has been described as a miscreant. He earned a dubious reputation as a scoundrel, criminal, and scalawag during the days of Reconstruction in North Carolina.

Before his arrival in Caswell County, Stephens drew the ire of many Conservatives—the opponents of Reconstruction—with his nefarious activities that exploited friends and family alike. In nearby Rockingham County, he was tagged with his infamous nickname, "Chicken," following a series of lawless incidents. He killed two chickens belonging to a neighbor after the animals had wandered on to his property. His subsequent arrest led to an overnight stay in jail. Once Stephens was released, he reacted like a madman by assaulting his neighbor with a stick. When two bystanders came to the aid of the hapless victim, Chicken pulled a pistol and shot both of them.

After settling in Yanceyville, Stephens continued this pattern of reprehensible behavior. In fact, in preparation for his relocation to Caswell County, he sold his mother's house without her knowledge and attempted to abandon her. His devious scheme was temporarily foiled when the unfortunate woman hunted him down in Caswell. However, soon after she moved in with her son, Chicken resorted to the ultimate solution. His mother's lifeless body was discovered beside her bed one morning. Her throat had been slit. According to her son, the mortal wound resulted from a fall onto a cracked chamber pot.

Despite his behavior, Stephens remained popular with the local political power brokers. In fact, he was appointed director of the Freedmen's Bureau by Judge Albion W. Tourgee. This new cloak of authority emboldened Chicken, who soon emerged as the alleged culprit and mastermind behind the destruction of barns, crops, and livestock on the farms of political opponents.

Even though the cause of the raging inferno that leveled the Yanceyville Hotel and a number of downtown structures was never proven, most fingers pointed at Stephens.

His reign of crime unchecked, Chicken proceeded to fix the 1868 election so that Judge Tourgee could hold his place on the bench. But more importantly, he ensured his own election to the state senate.

In Raleigh, Chicken had a political ally in Governor William W. Holden. Because of threatened violence by the Ku Klux Klan in Caswell and surrounding counties, the governor, at the request of Stephens and other Republican leaders, prevailed upon the legislature to consider a bill that would give Holden the power to suspend the writ of habeas corpus. When news of the potential loss of the basic freedom from unlawful restraint made its way into the hinterlands, many law-abiding citizens were outraged. Death threats were communicated to a number of Republican senators. One fled to the Midwest, but Chicken, although alarmed, was not about to leave his base of power in Caswell County. Rather, he turned his house into a fort and carried three firearms at all times. And just in case, he purchased a substantial insurance policy on his life.

As it turned out, no amount of protection would have saved Chicken from his fate. There were simply too many people out to do him in.

Some of his most ardent detractors formulated a secret plan to permanently rid the county of this menace. Their grand scheme was put into action on May 21, 1870, at the Caswell County Courthouse, which stood almost within sight of Chicken's residence. On that day, Conservatives gathered in the courtroom on the second floor to select their candidates for the upcoming election in August. State Senator Stephens happened to be in the courthouse at the time. At the direction of Frank Wiley, a former county sheriff, he went to a small office on the first floor. It was in this room that Chicken had once operated the Freedmen's Bureau.

Chicken was unsuspecting of Wiley because the senator had recently been in conversation with him concerning another run for sheriff. Nonetheless, when he walked into the room, which was then being used for wood storage, Stephens found three angry conspirators waiting to kill him. James Denny, one of the trio, suddenly had second thoughts, walked out of the room, and informed Wiley that the job was not yet finished. Incensed by the turn of events, Wiley grabbed John G. Lea, a local leader of the Ku Klux Klan, and screamed, "You must do something! I am exposed unless you do!" Lea was only too happy to oblige. He and approximately eight of his associates stormed into the room, where they promptly strangled and stabbed Stephens to death. After finishing their deadly business, the men left the room and locked the door behind them. The key was disposed of in County Line Creek.

A search party composed of the senator's two brothers and some friends began looking for Chicken after he failed to show up for the evening meal. Once they had scoured the downtown area—including the accessible portions of the courthouse—the men called off the search until daybreak. When they peeped in the window of the locked room at the courthouse the next morning, they were appalled to see Stephens's body in a fetal position on top of the stacked wood.

No one was ever convicted of the crime. It was not until the death of John Lea, the last surviving member of the band of killers, that the details of Chicken's murder were made public. Lea's sealed nine-page affidavit, opened after he was buried, provided the gory details of the revenge exacted on the senator.

In the wake of the murder, Governor Holden dispatched a three-hundred-man militia force to Caswell County to subdue subversive activities and arrest disloyal activists. The force was headed by a former Confederate deserter, the infamous George W. Kirk. By the time the soldiers arrived in Yanceyville, they realized that things were out of hand. The pendulum had swung in favor of the Conservatives. Most folks seemed to believe that Chicken Stephens had received a fair measure of justice.

As for Governor Holden, the citizens of North Carolina soon took care of him in a less violent fashion. After he was convicted of six counts of subverting the laws of the state, he was impeached on March 22, 1871, making him just the second governor so removed from office in United States history.

Should you visit the historic courthouse at Yanceyville, you can see the room where Chicken Stephens worked and died. But take care if the door closes behind you, for the ghost of the senator—which is said to visit the room on occasion—may very well be the responsible party. Why the ghost comes and goes from this room is unknown. Perhaps it is simply haunting the office where Stephens worked as agent for the Freedmen's Bureau. Or maybe it is seeking justice by searching for the murderers. In either case, beware! Perhaps the ghost is anxious to continue the misdeeds that were the hallmark of the late senator.

A Promise Kept

She was a Phantom of delight
When first she gleaned upon my sight;
A lovely apparition sent
To be a moment's ornament.

William Wordsworth

Chatham County is known as the home of one of the most haunted spots in all of America—the Devil's Tramping Ground. According to Tar Heel folklore, this eerie earthen circle forty feet in diameter is the work of the devil himself, who paces the isolated place on a regular basis. For as long as anyone can remember, no vegetation has grown in the circle, and all foreign objects placed in it mysteriously disappear overnight.

A variety of lesser known, yet highly intriguing, supernatural sites are also located in Chatham County. One such site, more romantic and less sinister than the Devil's Tramping Ground, is in Pittsboro, the venerable county seat. In the heart of the stately, old town stands the Hardin House, one of the most historic dwellings in Pittsboro. Built around 1838 by William Hardin, a prominent town commissioner, the house has long boasted well-landscaped lawns. Its backyard gracefully slopes to a picturesque spring where a promise was made between two lovers many, many years ago. As the legend goes, the apparition of one of the lovers frequents the spring on moonlit nights as she searches for her fiancé.

On a warm, wonderful spring evening in May 1839, all was right with the world, at least in the eyes of Philip Jones, a young Chatham County planter, and Helen Hardin. As the bright moon cast its glow on her golden hair and her flowing white dress, Helen hurried from the Hardin House to the springhouse where Philip, the love of her life, was waiting. There, the spring night was filled with the sweet smell of flowers.

His face beaming, the courtier greeted Helen with a compliment and a request: "Why, you're just like an angel. Promise that you will always stay the way you are tonight."

With schoolgirl shyness, the beautiful young woman answered softly, "I promise."

Almost as soon as she had said it, Helen suffered a brief dizzy spell. Alarmed when she momentarily lost her balance, Philip reached to steady her. Helen quickly regained her composure. Sensing Philip's anxiety, she sought to reassure him with words of hope and promise: "It is nothing. Perhaps I ran too fast to meet you. And then, too, I'm so happy to think that I, Helen Randolph Hardin, next month, June 1839, will become the wife of Mr. Philip Jones."

Their anxious moment gave way to laughter as Helen described the beauty of the gown she would wear on their wedding day. It was her grandmother's dress, which had come with the family from Ireland.

After they discussed the forthcoming parties related to the

wedding, Philip shared his excitement about the progress that he had made in restoring the house in which the newlyweds would live. He predicted that the summer would yield a bountiful crop and a handsome income for the couple.

The night was theirs. Each drank cool spring water from a gourd held by the other. They tossed coins into the water. With each coin went a special wish.

Suddenly, the spell was broken by the call of William Hardin: "Bedtime, daughter!"

Before parting, they shared a loving embrace and a long, romantic kiss. Then Helen bade Philip farewell at the springhouse, telling him she would walk back to the house alone because of the lateness of the hour. Philip agreed reluctantly.

As he watched Helen reach the crest of the hill, a dark cloud floated in front of the moon. Philip felt a sudden chill. When he lost sight of her, he made his way home. Little did he know that their wedding dreams were about to become a nightmare.

That night, Helen fell into a sleep from which she never awoke. The family doctor said it was a heart attack.

In his anguish, Philip returned to the springhouse night after night. There, he watched and waited for his dear Helen to come running down the hill into his waiting arms. Neighbors considered his behavior strange until someone reported seeing the vision of a young lady with golden tresses and a beautiful white dress near the spring on moonlit nights.

Over time, the Hardin family conveyed the house to St. Bartholomew's Episcopal Church for use as a rectory. However, sightings of the apparition continued.

The house changed hands again in the first decade of the twentieth century, when it was sold to William E. Brooks, the register of deeds of Chatham County. Townspeople reported seeing the figure of a lady at the spring behind the house. One frequent observer was Scotland Scurlock, a black servant who had to pass by the spring on his way home from work each night. Scurlock swore that on moonlit evenings, particularly in June, a young lady attired in a white dress would make her way down the hill from the Hardin House to the spring, then vanish.

Even today, there are reports that Helen makes her appearance at the spring when the moon shines brightly on warm spring nights. After all, she made a promise to Philip long ago. And ever since that time, she has remained true to that promise.

"Free! Oh, Free!"

We do not easily suspect evil of those whom we love most.

Peter Abélard

Fayetteville, one of the oldest and most historic cities in North Carolina, owed much of its early prominence to the mighty Cape Fear River, which courses through its corporate limits. Chartered in 1762, the city is located at the head of navigation on the river. In the nineteenth century, passenger steamboats connected Fayetteville with Wilmington and other ports and towns downriver.

The ghost of a pretty young woman who lived in Fayetteville in 1858 during the days of river travel is said to continue to walk the banks of the Cape Fear. Her name was Louisa, and she resided on the small farm of the uncle who reared her from childhood. Alas, Louisa's family was quite poor. Her uncle eked out a meager existence by growing sugarcane on the dark, fertile bottom land along the river.

On a nearby plantation was a handsome young overseer of slaves. Freeman, as he was named, was the son of aristocratic parents with whom he had a broken relationship. Louisa and Freeman met and soon began to see each other on a regular basis. Louisa's uncle disapproved of the courtship and warned his niece to stay away from "Free," as she called him, because the boy was no good. Unfortunately, the admonition came too late, for Louisa was already deeply in love with him.

As twilight drew the curtain on a splendid afternoon, the two lovers decided to take a walk along the river. In the course of their romantic stroll, the sweet Louisa informed Free that she was with child. She insisted that they make immediate plans for a wedding in order to avoid public disgrace. Free was shocked at the news but was willing to marry her.

But fate cruelly intervened the next morning. Free's father called on him at the plantation where the young man worked. The forgiving patriarch invited his prodigal son to return home to the lavish lifestyle he had enjoyed prior to their family disagreement. Elated by the sudden change in his fortune, Free planned to make the long trip home the following day. But before he departed, there was a problem he had to address.

Once again, Free and Louisa met at the river and walked the path where they had spent many an enchanted evening. Free apparently informed her of his reconciliation with his parents and his plan to return home, because the young woman was heard by a passerby to exclaim, "But you wouldn't come back. If you refuse, I shall go to your father and tell him the truth tonight. I can't face Uncle."

At first light the next day, Free and his parents left Fayetteville without telling anyone their destination. When the time came for Louisa to arise, her uncle was dismayed to discover her bed empty. He went to the plantation to find Free in the vain hope that Louisa might be with him. Upon learning that Free had left for parts unknown, the worried man made a desperate but un-successful attempt to locate him.

Three days later, the uncle's greatest fears were realized. Some men found Louisa's body floating against a log in the dark waters of the Cape Fear. Her corpse was tangled in yellow jessa-mine and honeysuckle vines. When authorities examined the corpse, they discovered a long, dark bruise across her forehead. She had died from blunt-force trauma.

Louisa was buried in a small family cemetery near the bank of the river where she had loved to walk with her dear Free. Following her burial, her uncle initiated a relentless search for her elusive lover. He successfully located the family's large plan-tation in South Carolina. According to Free's father, the young man had gone to Texas.

Because of limited resources, the uncle was forced to return to Fayetteville. Then the War Between the States ensued, render-ing a trip to Texas impossible. Once the conflict was over, Louisa's uncle did indeed visit the Lone Star State in his quest to bring Free to justice. There, he was given the news: Free had fought gallantly and died nobly as a soldier in the army of the Confed-erate States of America. In Texas, he left behind a lonely widow and a tiny son.

And what of Louisa and the unborn child she carried? Not long after her death, reports began to circulate that the appari-tion of a pretty young woman tangled in vines could be seen along the bank of the Cape Fear. To this day, the ghost of Louisa floats about the lane where she and her beau strolled in the twi-light of antebellum days. Should you walk that ancient lovers' lane as the light of the afternoon greets the gray of the evening, do not be alarmed if you hear the heartbroken voice of a melan-choly ghost cry out, "Free! Oh, Free!"

Guardians of the King's Treasure

Your lot is with the ghosts of soldiers dead.

Siegfried Sassoon

Abbotts Creek, a scenic and historic waterway, rises in northeastern Davidson County and flows diagonally through the county until it widens dramatically before emptying into the Yadkin River. A bridge spans the creek two miles east of Lexington, the seat of Davidson, at a place called Crotts Crossing. For more than two hundred years, ghostly creatures and supernatural occurrences have been reported at the creek in the vicinity of this ancient crossing.

For as long as anyone can remember, the eerie sights and sounds of Abbotts Creek have been attributed to a visit by Lord Charles Cornwallis and his red-coated army during the winter of 1781 in his quest to catch and destroy Major General Nathanael Greene and the battered American army of the South. Although Cornwallis camped alongside Abbotts Creek for but a brief period before he resumed his chase, it is said that the ghosts of several of his soldiers linger here to patrol the creek.

In the last week of January 1781, the famous British general formalized his plan to pursue General Greene and his beleaguered band of Americans while the Redcoats were encamped in Lincoln County at Ramsour's Mill, the site of a significant Patriot victory seven months earlier. During his brief sojourn at that battlefield, Cornwallis made one of the most fateful decisions of his campaign in the Carolinas. In direct contravention to standard European military practice, he directed that all of his army's expendable baggage—including large quantities of rum—be burned. Many of his wagons—beginning with his own—were torched. Only those carrying salt, medicine, ammunition, and gold and silver were spared. Cornwallis reasoned that he must lighten his army to hasten the pursuit of the Americans.

When a courier delivered the news of Cornwallis's decision to Nathanael Greene, the American general proclaimed words that would prove prophetic: "Then he is ours!" Then providence—or nature, at least—intervened on the side of the Americans. After Cornwallis moved his soldiers east from Lincoln County, he was twice delayed when heavy rains gorged the Catawba and the Yadkin Rivers and rendered them temporarily impassable. Greene and his ragged troops fled for their lives, narrowly escaping the clutches of the lightened British army over the several weeks that followed.

When Cornwallis was finally able to move his troops across the Yadkin, he camped at Abbotts Creek in the early days of February 1781. Upon learning that Greene had recently bivouacked nearby, the British commander sensed that he was now within reach of his prey. Should he be able to annihilate or capture Greene's forces, the rebellion in the South would be extinguished, and the American Revolution would be over. His Majesty, King George III, would once again reign over the insurgent colonies.

Driven by the expectation that complete victory was within

his grasp, Cornwallis decided to further lighten his load while his army rested here along the creek. To move his warriors with all due speed toward a showdown with Greene, heavy barrels of gold and silver coins from the king's treasury were pulled from the British wagon train under cover of darkness and rolled into the dark waters of Abbotts Creek.

As far as anyone knows, the treasure has never been recovered. Since an apparent wealth of gold and silver awaits discovery, it is curious that the creek has not been besieged by fortune hunters over the years. Area residents, however, can readily explain why the king's treasure remains safely hidden more than two centuries after it was dropped into the water for safekeeping: ghosts roam the creek and its banks as guardians of the British riches.

From the time that Cornwallis departed the area to the present day, the ghosts of Abbotts Creek have been seen and heard by countless persons. They appear as strange lights that float along the still, shimmering water of the creek, up its banks, and into the adjacent forests at the very point where the Redcoats crossed the waterway. Local legend has it that no treasure seeker has ever been bold enough to confront the ghosts.

The residents of Crotts Crossing have been reared on spine-chilling tales of encounters with unknown entities from the near and distant past. At times, headless figures have suddenly materialized to accompany unwitting persons strolling the creek banks. On one occasion, a man rode his horse to the spot where the barrels of coins were said to have been rolled into the creek. Without warning, something jumped on the animal behind the rider. The man and his mount were so frightened that they ran in terror. In the midst of their flight, the ghostly form vanished into thin air. No other plausible explanation being available, that phantom is said to have been the ghost of a sentry assigned to protect Cornwallis's cache.

During the Civil War, an unusual confrontation took place along the road near the existing bridge. A local man on foot came upon a stranger who refused to identify himself or to step aside so that the man could pass. Vexed by the stranger's discourteous behavior and suspicious of his intentions, the man swung a heavy hammer at him, only to see it pass completely through the body of the intended victim. The stranger then cast a horrifying glare and displayed an ominous grin before vanishing before the eyes of the stunned fellow.

Many of the reports of supernatural happenings at Abbotts Creek have come from local opossum hunters. On occasion, woodsmen have become hopelessly lost during night hunts in the forests bordering the creek and have not been able to find their way out until the light of day. Few of these hunters have ever been willing to venture into the forests again because of the ghosts they witnessed. Expensive, well-trained opossum dogs have led these hunters to trees and barked furiously to signal that the prey was located. Alas, when the men climbed the trees, nothing was to be found. Time after time, trusted, faithful hunting dogs have thus chased the phantoms of Abbotts Creek.

One of the community's most reputable citizens witnessed the terror experienced by his reliable opossum dogs, Cash and Means. As he rode toward his father's home one evening, the young man followed his dogs as they were attracted to a persimmon tree near the creek. With a full moon providing light on the pitch-black night, the hunter saw what he perceived to be a plump, meaty opossum on a high tree limb. He tied his horse and quickly made his way up the tree, where he spied what he thought was a grinning opossum. But when he shook the "animal" from the limb, Cash and Means were stricken with fright. For the duration of the night, the normally fearless dogs refused to leave the sight of their owner. Once again, the ghosts of Abbotts Creek had deceived both man and animal.

Eerie noises have been heard here, too. Generations of area residents have been disturbed by the unmistakable sound of a barrel rolling down the bank and splashing into Abbotts Creek. These strange sounds have been heard at all hours of the day but are most often experienced at night. A well-known and much-respected local justice of the peace once hurried to the creek after he heard a barrel of coins rolling through the woods and bumping over rocks and stumps as it made its way toward the water. Rushing to the water's edge, he expected to witness a splash or at least the resulting ripples. He saw neither. The venerable jurist noted that the strange occurrence caused his white hair to stand on end.

It has been surmised that the sounds of the phantom barrels are intended to frighten away those who would discover the treasure. On at least one occasion, the bizarre sounds accomplished their purpose. One summer day, a group of men who were either unaware of the ghosts or who did not believe the stories decided to go swimming au naturel in the creek near the site of the Revolutionary War crossing. No sooner had the bathers begun enjoying the cool, refreshing water than the ghosts started their mischief. Phantom barrel after phantom barrel came rolling down the hill with a thunderous roar. But none of the swimmers could see the source of the mysterious disturbance. So terrified were they that they scrambled from the creek, put on scant clothing, and fled from the area, never to return.

When Cornwallis crossed Abbotts Creek during the first week of February 1781, he surrendered to its waters the riches of his army in the vain hope of conquering the enemy. As fate would have it, he himself was subdued eight months later and surrendered his sword to a triumphant American army. In time, the general and his defeated soldiers sailed home to Great Britain.

Nonetheless, should you have occasion to visit the historic crossing at Abbotts Creek, beware of the ghosts of the men Cornwallis left behind. Even after the passage of so many years, these dutiful ghostly guardians continue to perform their assigned task. The king's treasure thus continues to lie undisturbed in its eighteenth-century hiding place.

Justice from beyond the Grave

The true mystery of the world is the visible, not the invisible.

Oscar Wilde

Over the last fifty years, as the television set has become an almost universal fixture in the American home, the popularity of the courtroom drama has never waned. From *Perry Mason* and *The Defenders* in the fifties and sixties to the myriad attorney programs on the current television schedule, these dramas have glamorized the lives of trial attorneys but have done little to present a realistic view of daily activities in the courtroom. Unlike the grueling tedium of real-life trials, the shows of this genre are invariably resolved by the appearance of a surprise or star witness out of the blue. Yet not even the incomparable Perry Mason—the most legendary of all attorneys on the screen—was able to win a case through evidence provided by a ghost. Nevertheless, that is just what happened in a celebrated legal proceeding in Davie County in 1925.

This true North Carolina trial drama has as its central character and its ghost Mr. James L. Chaffin. During the first two decades of the twentieth century, Chaffin lived with his wife and four sons—John, James Pinkney, Marshall, and Abner—on a farm several miles from Mocksville, the seat of Davie County. In the summer of 1921, Chaffin suffered a serious fall that proved to be fatal. In the wake of his tragic death, his will—duly executed and attested by two witnesses on November 16, 1905—was probated at the courthouse in Mocksville. For reasons not specified in the document, Chaffin left all his property to his third son, Marshall, and made no provisions whatsoever for his wife or other three sons. Although the disinherited family members were chagrined and hurt, they could find no legal grounds to file a caveat to the will or to challenge its authenticity.

The Chaffin family seemed to be making significant progress in healing its wounds until the day in 1922 when Marshall died. Under the terms of his estate, all of the property he had inherited from his father—including the Chaffin farm—went to his wife and minor son. Though this disposition inflamed the family sensitivities, there seemed to be nothing that Mrs. Chaffin and her three disinherited sons could do. But things were to change four years later with the appearance of the ghost of James L. Chaffin.

The ghost of the family patriarch began manifesting itself to the second son, James Pinkney Chaffin, in early 1925. As a result of the spirit's nocturnal visits over the course of several months, young Chaffin made his way to Mocksville in June during the busy farm season to file a lawsuit, in which he challenged the validity of his father's will of 1905. By the time *Chaffin v. Chaffin* came to trial in mid-December 1925, the case had attracted the attention of legal scholars as well as laymen because of the strange allegations made by the widow and three sons.

When James Pinkney Chaffin took the witness stand, the

courtroom was packed. He began his testimony by offering a rather bizarre tale: "In all my life, I never heard my father mention having made a later will than the one dated in 1905. But some months ago, I began to have vivid dreams, in which my father appeared at my bedside. At first, he did not say anything. He just stood there and looked at me with a sorrowful expression. He seemed to have something on his mind—as if he felt that, in his lifetime, he had done something wrong and wished that he could set it right." The witness then expressed to the court his longstanding belief that his father had not done right when he left everything to Marshall. However, Pinkney had not initially equated that problem with the appearance of his father's ghost. "It did not occur to me that this could be what was worrying him," he testified. "I did not attach any importance to it."

Then came the night when the ghost was costumed in the same black overcoat that the elder Chaffin had worn in his lifetime. Pinkney explained to the court that the apparition of his father had moved close to the bed, pulled back the overcoat, pointed to the inside pocket, and said, "You will find something about my last will in my overcoat pocket." With those words, the ghost had vanished. Pinkney woke up the next morning convinced that he had not dreamed the encounter. He noted in his testimony, "I was sure that my father's spirit had come back from the grave and spoken to me." Acting upon the instructions supplied by the ghost, Pinkney had asked his mother about his father's old overcoat. When she informed him that the garment had been given to his older brother, he made a hasty twenty-mile trip to the farm residence of John Chaffin in nearby Yadkin County.

After Pinkney told his brother the story of their father's most recent visit, the two took the overcoat from the closet with the expectation of finding a will. Pinkney's testimony revealed what they discovered instead: "When I examined the inside pocket, I found the lining had been stitched to the coat. I cut the stitches, and inside the lining was a little roll of paper tied with a string. Written on that piece of paper, in my father's handwriting, were these words: 'Read the twenty-seventh chapter of Genesis in my daddy's old Bible.' "

Pinkney promptly started out on the journey back to his mother's, where his grandfather's Bible was located. In the course of that trip, he realized that it might be prudent to have an impartial witness on hand when he examined the Bible. To that end, he persuaded a neighbor, James Blackwelder, to accompany him.

Mrs. Chaffin could not readily put her hands on the Bible. After an exhaustive search, it was finally located in a chest in the attic. With his mother, his wife, his teenage daughter, and Blackwelder looking on, Pinkney picked up the Bible. He described to the court what happened next: "The Bible was in bad shape, and while I was handling it, it fell into three pieces. Mr. Blackwelder picked up the part containing the book of Genesis and turned the leaves with the twenty-seventh chapter. At that place, two leaves had been folded together, forming a pocket." And there it was—James L. Chaffin's last will and testament. Introduced into evidence at the trial, it read,

> After reading the 27th chapter of Genesis, I, James L. Chaffin, do make my last will and testament and here it is. I want, after giving my body a decent burial, my little property to be equally divided among my four children, if they are living at my death, both personal and real estate divided equal; if not living, share to their children. And if she is living, you must take care of your mammy. Now this is my last will and testament. Witness my hand and seal.
>
> James L. Chaffin
> This January 16, 1919

Even though the handwritten will was not witnessed, it was valid under state law because several witnesses offered testimony that it bore the handwriting of James L. Chaffin.

After the will was presented, the twenty-seventh chapter of Genesis—which chronicles how Esau was tricked out of his birthright by Jacob—was read to the court.

By that point in the trial, Marshall's widow had heard and seen enough. Before the matter could be submitted to the jury, the parties reached a settlement.

At the conclusion of the legal proceedings, skeptics descended upon Mocksville after reading accounts of Mr. Chaffin's ghost. Pinkney was quick to respond to the doubters: "Many of my friends do not believe that it is possible for the living to hold communication with the dead, but I am convinced that my father actually appeared to me on several occasions—and I'll believe it to the day of my death."

Indeed, Pinkney had experienced a final encounter with the ghost about a week before the trial began. It had convinced him that he should follow through with the lawsuit. He had ended his courtroom testimony with these words: "About a week ago, my father appeared to me again in a dream. He showed considerable temper and asked, 'Where is my old will?' From that, I concluded he hoped I would win the suit."

Sooner or later, a television courtroom drama will reach its denouement through evidence supplied by a ghost. Before you dismiss that fictional dramatization as pure poppycock, recall this unusual case from Davie County, in which North Carolina jurisprudence allowed a ghost to ensure that justice was served.

All for the
Love of Gold

Alas, then the sun goes in again, and we are back in the kingdom of fantasy, where it is goodness that is flat and boring, and evil that is varied and attractive, profound, intriguing, and full of charm.

Malcolm Muggeridge

In the early eighteenth century, the Old Horn Inn was a welcome sight for weary travelers along the red-clay road that is now US 70 leading from Durham to Hillsborough. Covered with wooden shakes, the two-story hostelry stood a few miles west of where the city of Durham is located today, near the present Durham County-Orange County line. Adjacent to the inn were extensive swamps and marshes extending from the banks of the Eno River.

To the delight of wayfarers, the tavern offered music and dancing in addition to shelter and sustenance. But when the lights were turned out and darkness engulfed the place, it took on a sinister ambience, thanks to the owner and operator, John Horn, a vile, ruthless, contemptible man whose physical appearance was as ugly as his character. His leathery skin, toughened by exposure to the elements, was similar to that of an alligator, and his scary, deceiving eyes were akin to those of a snake.

In stark contrast to Old John Horn was his charming daughter, Elizabeth. Blessed with a beauty as rare as the most precious jewel, she had alluring blue eyes, flowing golden brown hair, and a sweet, winning smile. Many patrons came simply to catch a glimpse of her. Elizabeth was shy around strangers. One of the reasons was the quality of the clientele that the inn attracted. Most guests were crude, poorly groomed ruffians. Elizabeth cringed when she laid eyes on them or heard the profane words that issued from their mouths.

One day, a man completely different from all the others rode up to the inn. From her vantage point on the veranda, Elizabeth reckoned that she had never beheld such a handsome person. He was young, tall, and muscular; underneath his cocked hat was beautiful, well-kept, raven-black hair; he wore a snow-white ruffled blouse and polished boots. After Jerry Mason hitched his horse, he looked up to catch Elizabeth Horn staring at him. At the moment his eyes met hers, she blushed and looked away. Jerry stepped onto the porch, his spurs clinking with every step. As he approached the big front door, Elizabeth, attired in an attractive blue dress, stepped aside for him to pass. Once again, their eyes met, this time for more than a fleeting moment. Here, truly, was love at first sight. Without introducing himself, without saying a word, Jerry gently took Elizabeth's hand, and they walked down the steps to the front lawn, where they gazed over the countryside in the twilight of a beautiful Carolina afternoon. Their hearts beat in unison as their beautiful romance—albeit ever so short, as this story shall reveal—blossomed.

Jerry sojourned at the inn. The couple spent cool mornings and sun-drenched afternoons in pleasant walks about the grounds. Moonlit nights brought affectionate embraces and kisses under a canopy of twinkling stars. Meanwhile, the wretched John Horn carefully monitored his young daughter and her suitor, his evil eyes affixed to Jerry Mason's gold-laden saddlebags.

One stormy night as thunder boomed along the Eno and lightning illuminated the otherwise dark inn, the unscrupulous innkeeper decided that the gold must be his. And to his way of thinking, there was only one way to make it his: he must kill Jerry Mason.

Everyone had long retired for the evening when Old John put his plan into action. Cracks of thunder muffled the sounds of the creaking steps as he made his way down to the kitchen. There, he selected the longest, sharpest butcher knife and secreted it under his coat. Armed for the heinous task before him, he made his way back up the steps toward the room assigned to Jerry Mason.

In a room down the hall, an unusually loud clap of thunder stirred Elizabeth from her slumber. She sprang upright in bed and screamed at the top of her lungs as the wind howled outside and the rain pelted her windows. An ominous feeling sent shivers up her spine. As she pulled the covers over her, she heard footsteps in the hall. Mustering every bit of her courage, Elizabeth arose from bed, ever so slowly opened the door, and peered into the dark hall. Seeing nothing, she decided to hasten to the safety of Jerry's room. His door was open. When Elizabeth turned to walk in, a flash of lightning illuminated the room. She was aghast at what she saw: her father held an upraised knife at Jerry's bedside! With the quickness of a cat, the girl flung herself between Old John and her beau.

Her attempt to prevent the terrible crime was seconds too late, for her father's knife was already covered with blood. Jerry did not respond to her frantic pleas to wake up. Reacting as if she had gone mad, Elizabeth began alternately laughing and crying while she sat on the bed bearing the bloody corpse. But when she noticed that Old John was still in the room, she rushed head-long toward him. John was waiting with a brutal hand, which bloodied his daughter's delicate face and sent her sprawling on the wooden floor. Before she could stand, the murderer gathered her in his arms, carried her to her room, and locked the door.

Anxious to gain her freedom, Elizabeth broke open a window and climbed out onto the sturdy limb of a massive oak tree. The storm still raged. As she hung suspended on the limb, she spotted the light of a lantern in the stable yard. It revealed Old John leading away a horse with a blanket-covered body draped across it. Elizabeth dropped from the tree and made a desperate attempt to ascertain where her father was taking Jerry's body. Screaming, she raced in the direction of the lantern and grabbed her father's arm. Old John reacted violently, subduing her by binding her with ropes. Then, with a lash of his whip, he sent the horse into the quicksand of the marsh. What better place to dispose of Jerry's body?

Elizabeth could only watch in horror as the unfortunate animal sank into the quagmire. But as the horse's head disappeared below the surface, she broke free from the hastily tied ropes and bolted toward the marsh. Before Old John could restrain her, she leaped into the quicksand. All her father's efforts to pull her from a certain death were refused. Elizabeth's final gurgles and the sounds of the rain, wind, and thunder combined in a symphony of the macabre.

At the very moment she vanished into the muck to join her lover, the storm stopped. Clouds floated away to reveal a pale, menacing moon. Old John was gripped with fear. Fleeing toward the inn, he shrieked in terror along the entire route. Once inside, he cowered in fear by the big fireplace.

In the days that followed, Old John attempted to ease his pain and loss by counting and recounting his ill-gotten treasure, the gold of Jerry Mason. But he could not erase from his mind the sights and sounds of the gruesome events.

His torment became horror when Elizabeth's ghost began to make nightly visits. She bore Jerry's splattered blood on her face.

One evening before the ghost made its regular appearance, another savage storm erupted. Old John again took refuge near the fireplace. As the storm raged, his mind began to play tricks on him—or so he thought. The dull, steady sound of the rain reminded him of the moans of a dying lady. Then, above the roar of the storm, he heard it—the unmistakable sound of a woman screaming. John covered his ears, but the scream only grew louder. Certain that it was Elizabeth, he scrambled to his feet and hurried out into the miserable night, leaving behind the gold he had been counting on the kitchen table.

No one ever saw Old John again, though someone found his hat floating in the quicksand the morning after the storm.

Elizabeth's ghost is said to have haunted the Old Horn Inn until it was torn down. But even today, if you should happen by the marshes along the Eno River on a stormy night, don't be surprised if you hear the haunting screams of pretty Elizabeth Horn—grim reminders of the night of evil that unfolded here many years ago.

Moravian Stars

And the stars of heaven fell unto the earth, even as a fig tree casteth her untimely figs, when she is shaken of mighty wind.

Revelation 6:13

From the beginning of time, stars have been held in awe as mystical heavenly bodies. A clear nighttime sky adorned with countless stars continues to fascinate North Carolinians of the twenty-first century, just as it did the first Tar Heels to behold the spectacle. For lovers, it represents the glory and splendor of romance; for dreamers, it offers a tangible piece of the illusory world they seek; for adventurers, it unveils a map to worlds yet to be explored; for scientists, it yields a tantalizing look at the boundless depths of space; and for the religious, it provides a glimpse of the wonder of creation.

For the Moravians, who have called the area that is now Forsyth County home since long before the county was established, a star-filled sky is a reminder of one of their most precious symbols, the Moravian Star. But it is also a reminder of that spooky night in the first half of the nineteenth century when thousands upon thousands of stars fell from the sky in full view of the horrified residents of the Moravian settlements in Forsyth County. No one really knows what happened on that terrifying night, perhaps the most frightening in the history of the state. Without a doubt, there has never been one like it since.

Each Christmas season, numerous homes throughout North Carolina and other parts of the United States are decorated with the beautiful, multi-pointed star of the Moravians, a group of European Protestants who came to America in 1734 in search of religious freedom. In 1753, the first of many Moravians from Pennsylvania settled in Wachovia, as the 98,985-acre tract owned by the denomination in North Carolina was known. From the day they put down roots here, the Moravians were meticulous record keepers. Historians owe an immeasurable debt of gratitude to these devoutly religious people for their tireless efforts to record events in North Carolina. From the diaries and other written records of the Moravians, we can today understand the fear that gripped the people of Wachovia and other North Carolinians on the night when it appeared that the earth would be no more.

By all accounts, November 12, 1833, was a bright, crisp, and very cool autumn day in the Moravian settlements of Wachovia. Residents of Bethabara, Bethania, and Salem were well aware that, on any clear night, the chance of catching sight of a falling star was great. These blazing celestial bodies were particularly noticeable during November because the Leonids, as they were known, radiated from the sickle-shaped group of stars in the constellation Leo. But no one in Wachovia or anywhere else in the state was prepared for what fell from the sky in the wee morning hours of November 13.

At Salem, the most famous of the Moravian settlements, the

church diary contains a description of the eerie events: "In the night of November 13, the weather being very clear and cold, there occurred a phenomenon of nature seldom seen here, for the so-called falling stars were observed in great numbers, in various sizes and shapes, and in all directions, this continued all night and until daylight made them invisible."

From the sandy shores of the Atlantic to the tallest peaks east of the Mississippi, stunned North Carolinians stumbled out of their beds and walked out into the darkness to watch in shock, fear, excitement, and utter disbelief. Alarm spread throughout the state because no one had ever observed such a terrifying display in the sky.

At Bethabara, the oldest of the villages in Wachovia, the Moravian church diary chronicled the panic occasioned by the rain of stars: "Before day there was an unusual appearance in our heavens, for, in the clear sky, when from a certain point, thousands of *feurer funken* [fire sparks] darted in all directions and portions of the sky, many people, especially among our neighbors, were so frightened that they believed the end of the world had come, and leaving their homes before day fled with their families to their neighbors, seeking protection."

The rain of stars was witnessed as far north as Canada, as far south as the West Indies, and as far west as the Rocky Mountains. A distinguished professor at Yale studied the events of the strange night. Based upon his research, he concluded that "the stars fell on that occasion like flakes of snow, to the number, it was estimated here, of 240,000 in the space of nine hours, varying in size from a point of phosphorescent light to globes of the moon's diameter."

One North Carolina planter was awakened from a deep slumber by what he termed "the most distressing cries that ever fell upon my ears." From outside the plantation house poured "shrieks of terror and mercy." Unsure of the cause of the ruckus, he armed himself with his sword and made his way to the veranda. There, he was unnerved to see a large number of his slaves lying on the lawn. Then he looked to the sky. His observations of that moment are telling: "Upwards of 100 lay prostrate on the ground, some speechless and some giving utterance to the bitterest cries. With hands upraised they implored God to save the world and them. The scene was truly awful for never did rain fall much thicker than the meteors fell toward the earth—east, west, north, south, it was all the same."

On the streets of Salem, one citizen observed that the falling stars seemed to cover the "whole heaven." The hysteria exhibited that night by the normally staid Moravians was something he had never before witnessed. "It looked like streaks of lightning and frightened more people than the [Revolutionary] war ever did," he recorded. "Christian Butner lived near Mickey's Mill. He ran two miles with his wife and children to his brother-in-law's—Mr. Stuthard, and getting there, could not speak for quite a while. The others were in the same fix and thought the last day had come."

What happened on November 13, 1833, when the Moravians and their fellow North Carolinians watched as the stars poured from the sky? Most likely, it was the greatest and heaviest meteor storm ever witnessed in America. Or just maybe it was something from the supernatural world. No one knows for sure. But one thing is for certain: no single event, supernatural or otherwise, has scared more Tar Heels than the night when the world seemed to be at an end. And no people of our state were more affected than the Moravians of Forsyth County, who, ironically, cherish their special star of the Yuletide season. One of their number put it best about that frightful night when he wrote, "The people in general were the worst frightened I ever knew them to be."

Lady in Blue

To me there is something thrilling and exalting in the thought that we are drifting forward into a splendid mystery— into something no mortal eye hath seen, and no intelligence has yet declared.

E. H. Chapin

Belford, a small community near the Franklin County-Nash County line, was born of an expansive plantation of the same name that once sprawled into both counties. Established in 1798 by David Sills, Belford Plantation was named for his former home in England. In 1822, the federal government opened a post office at Belford. Shortly thereafter, the plantation became a popular stopover on the stagecoach route from Philadelphia to Savannah. During its days as a welcome respite for travelers, the place acquired the ghost of a mysterious woman known as the Lady in Blue.

On New Year's Eve in 1835, the Savannah-bound stage pulled into Belford Plantation in the midst of a freak, savage thunderstorm. Although it was winter, continuous claps of thunder disturbed the night and wicked streaks of lightning illuminated the sky. A heavy, wind-driven rain severely impeded visibility, rendering further travel impossible that evening. To make matters worse, one of the three passengers—a frail, middle-aged lady attired in a royal blue suit complete with veil—was seriously ill. She had suffered a seizure and lapsed into unconsciousness during the journey.

As soon as the driver pulled the stage alongside the plantation post office, Dr. Grey Sills, then the owner of Belford, greeted the new arrivals. Upon being informed of the distressed condition of the female passenger, Dr. Sills directed his servants to carry the lady into the right front guest room on the second floor of the plantation house. There, the physician labored to save his patient. But despite his best efforts, the woman expired exactly at the stroke of midnight. All the while, the storm raged outside. But five minutes after her death, the tempest ended as suddenly as it had started.

Dr. Sills remained at the bedside and examined the corpse in a vain attempt to locate some identification, so as to be able to notify her next of kin. Finding none, he questioned the coach driver and his assistant about the lady dressed in blue. His inquiry yielded some information: the woman had boarded the stage alone in Philadelphia; her passage had been paid by the Overland Stage Company; and she had engaged in very little conversation with the other passengers on the trip south.

The following morning, Dr. Sills, convinced that the deceased woman's identity would likely remain a mystery, made preparations for her funeral and her burial at the Belford Church Cemetery. She was interred in the same blue suit she was wearing when she died.

In subsequent years, the stage driver made it a point to stop overnight at Belford Plantation. On each occasion, he discussed the stormy night involving the mysterious Lady in Blue. It was during this same time that a number of sightings of an eerie, blue-clad woman with a bluish complexion were reported about the grounds of Belford.

Dr. Sills dismissed these reports as pure fiction until the afternoon that he and some friends were scouting the plantation on horseback in search of a site on which to build a new chapel. All of a sudden, a ghostly woman dressed in blue was standing beside them. A startling noise caused the men to look away. When they turned back to check on the strange woman, she was gone. A thorough search of the surrounding woodlands and thickets yielded no trace of the apparition.

Days later, Mary Louise Sills, the doctor's daughter, was enjoying a carriage ride with her friends when they were confronted by a phantom in blue. She appeared in front of the horses out of nowhere. As in the incident witnessed by Dr. Sills, a loud, unusual noise momentarily distracted the occupants of the carriage. When they again turned their attention to the spooky woman, she had vanished.

In 1857, Dr. Sills donated a parcel of land for the construction of the chapel that later became Belford Church. The chapel straddled the county line—the altar was in Nash County and the front door in Franklin County. Just after the Civil War, a man from nearby Castalia happened upon the church late one night. He found it curious that the lights inside were burning. As he drew closer, he was surprised to find horses and buggies hitched outside the building. Upon hearing hymns being sung, he peered in a window. Inside were people in the pews, and in the pulpit, leading the singing, was a lady dressed in blue. Deciding to join the worshipers, the man jumped down from his horse, hitched it, removed his hat, and opened the front door. As soon as he entered, darkness engulfed the sanctuary, and the singing ceased. He hurriedly fetched his lantern and held it up to ascertain what was going on. The light disclosed that there was no one else in the church. Unnerved, the fellow hurried outside, where there was but one horse tied to the hitching post.

Succeeding generations of the Sills family also had unexplained encounters with the Lady in Blue. Most family members were of the belief that the apparition of the mystery lady was forced to wander Belford because it could not get home.

In the first third of the twentieth century, the Sills family sold the plantation and moved to nearby Nashville. And then it happened. About nine o'clock on New Year's Eve in 1935, a violent thunderstorm struck the Belford area. It was much like the one the night the Lady in Blue arrived. Horrific winds uprooted trees as the storm grew in fury. Area residents say that it reached its maximum intensity at the very stroke of midnight. Just then, a jagged bolt of lightning hit the plantation house, which had been vacant for almost a year. In a matter of minutes, the resulting fire reduced the historic structure to smoldering ruins. At half-past midnight, the storm ended and the skies cleared.

When the morning sun brought light to Belford, two chimneys standing like sentinels over the ashes of the once-grand estate were all that remained. An examination of the ruins revealed that the fire had started in the very bedroom where the Lady in Blue had died exactly one hundred years ago to the very second. Following the fire, the phantom vanished as mysteriously as the Lady in Blue had arrived a century earlier.

The Drip, Drip, Drip of Dark Blue Blood

I wants to make your flesh creep.

Charles Dickens

Mount Holly, a town located in eastern Gaston County on the western bank of the Catawba River, is the site of one of the most terrifying haunted houses in North Carolina. To protect the privacy of the owners, the exact location of the nineteenth-century dwelling—known as the Wilson House for the purposes of this story—and the names of its occupants, both past and present, will not be given here. However, this chilling tale is based upon fact and eyewitness accounts.

Not only is the haunt in the Wilson House one of the most frightening in the state, it is also the most consistent. The gruesome thing appears but one day—or one night, that is—every year, and that is October 25.

It was on the cold, damp night of October 25, 1886, when the hideous creature first appeared. A bone-chilling rain was pouring down when George Wilson and his wife, Mathilda, pulled up to the front entrance of their Mount Holly residence in a horse-drawn carriage. The hour was late—an hour before mid-night, to be exact—and the couple was very tired after a journey to visit Mathilda's ailing mother. As soon as Mathilda reached the shelter of the expansive veranda, George proceeded toward the barn with the horse and buggy. En route, he heard a horrible scream from his wife. His heart in his throat, George leaped from the carriage and raced into the house. He found a pale Mathilda lying at the foot of the stairs in the foyer, which was bathed in an eerie, blue light. George reckoned that she had fainted.

And then, suddenly, he found out why. He heard an unearthly moan from the second floor. When he looked to the top of the stairs, sheer terror gripped him, for there stood a ghastly apparition giving off a blue light that flooded the entrance hall. From George's vantage point, the thing appeared to be a man in uniform, possibly Confederate. Yet the creature had no eyes, but only dark, sunken circles. Even more frightening was its left arm. There was no hand, but rather a stub, and it dripped dark blue blood.

So horrified was George that he could not move. Then the hideous thing took a step and raised its right arm, as if it were coming after George. Mustering every ounce of his courage, the master of the house lifted Mathilda into his arms, ran out into the dark night, and headed in the direction of the barn.

The cold rain that fell upon her face revived Mathilda. George gently laid her on a bale of hay in the relative safety of the barn and held her close in an attempt to console her. After a short time, he left her side momentarily to walk to the barn door to ascertain what was going on in the house. He stood there aghast as the blue light moved through the dwelling. George decided it best that he and Mathilda remain in the barn until daybreak.

George Wilson was a literate man who had maintained a day-book for many years. In it, he recorded the weather, his business matters, and events of daily import. On October 26, 1886, George ended his daybook entry on an ominous note: "We will possibly never spend another night in our home."

Over the three weeks that followed, the Wilsons lived with Mathilda's parents. But George grew weary of traveling to and fro to take care of his farm. At length, he decided to brave his house once again.

On November 16, he wrote this in his journal: "Tonite I shall risk a night at home. I shall see if the ghost returns."

Two days later, George noted that he had stayed in the house on the nights of November 16 and 17 without encountering the creature. His entry concluded, "Tomorrow Mathilda has agreed to move back home."

Over the next year, things returned to normal. Then came October 25. Before he retired for the evening, George made the following routine observation in his daybook: "Today is the earliest freeze anyone can recall."

About eleven o'clock that cold night, George was startled from a deep sleep. He sat straight up in bed and squinted at the doorway. The ominous blue light had returned. Too afraid to move, George pulled closer to the sleeping Mathilda, so as to protect her from the unknown visitor.

In a few moments, the blue light disappeared from the doorway. But all was not well. There was the unmistakable sound of footsteps on the stairs. George knew that the ghost was making its way down to the first floor. For more than an hour, he listened from the bed as the phantom opened cabinets and drawers, apparently in search of something.

All of the commotion on the first floor woke Mathilda. Initially, she thought that a burglar was ransacking the house, but when she gazed into her husband's eyes, she knew that the malevolent menace had returned. Mathilda's bloodcurdling scream reverberated through the house, but the noise downstairs continued unabated.

George and Mathilda held each other tight the rest of the night. They were not harmed. At first light, the terrified couple ventured from their bedroom. After a careful search of the house, they began to pack their belongings. In shaky handwriting unlike that of happier days, George logged his final daybook entry on October 26, 1887: "Something evil has driven us from our home."

With those words, George and Mathilda left forever. For almost a half-dozen years, the place remained vacant, during which time it acquired a local reputation as a haunted house.

When members of a Tennessee family, the Ansons, moved to Mount Holly in the mid-1890s, they made the mistake of buying the Wilson House. Although no one publicly reported any visits by the creature during the family's twenty-year residence, the circumstances surrounding the death of Will Anson—which occurred, oddly enough, on October 25, 1913—are quite mysterious. Will, the master of the house, died that day of a heart attack at the age of forty-two. What caused the attack was never recorded, but it is curious that on the following day, Susannah, Will's wife, departed for Tennessee with the children and all of the family's belongings. Neither she nor the children returned to Mount Holly for Will's funeral.

For the next ten years, the Wilson House stood empty. In 1923, it was purchased at a tax sale by Sam and Martha Blake. After extensively remodeling and modernizing the residence, the Blakes moved there in early September 1926. But their excitement soon turned to terror.

As Sam ascended the stairs to retire for the evening on October 25, 1926, he thought to himself how unusually warm the night was. Yet when he reached the top of the steps, he encountered a strange cold spot. As he and his wife prepared for bed, Martha remarked that she had experienced the same cold feeling.

Around eleven o'clock, Sam awoke to the sound of moaning. He saw a bluish glow at the bedroom door and got up to determine what was going on. When he gazed down the hallway, he saw the creature that had haunted the house for some fifty years. As he stood motionless in the doorway, the thing with no eyes and a handless left arm dripping liquid began making its way down the stairs. The third step creaked.

Convinced that a robber had invaded the house, Sam took his gun from the bedroom closet and dashed into the hallway. As he took aim, he felt something warm and sticky on his bare feet. Dropping his rifle, he saw blue blood on the floor. Scared out of his wits, Sam ran back into the bedroom and slammed the door behind him.

Awakened by the disturbance, Martha wanted to know what was going on. When Sam assured her that all was well, she fell back into slumber. But Sam couldn't sleep. He listened in fear as the thing searched the drawers and cabinets downstairs.

When Martha arose the following morning, Sam related the terrifying events of the night. Much like the Wilsons, the Blakes moved out for a time before deciding to try it again. Upon their return, the wary couple discovered broken dishes and glassware in the cupboard. Upstairs, they made an even more startling discovery: blood spots at the top of the stairway. When all attempts to remove the stains proved vain, the Blakes placed a rug over that portion of the floor. To their dismay, the blood spots showed up on the rug. They called in a carpenter to tear up the stained flooring and to replace it with new wood. No sooner had he laid the new floor than the blood spots appeared again. To this day, they remain.

The Blakes spent the next October 25 in the house. After the creature paid a return visit that night, Sam and Martha moved away for good.

Since that time, the house has been occupied by a number

of families. On October 25, 1964, the Simpson family had its first experience with the thing. The Simpsons' description of the creature and its nocturnal activities matched exactly that provided by George Wilson more than seventy-five years earlier.

In more recent times, the residents of the house have developed a peaceful way to coexist with the bluish ghost. Each year, they simply spend the night of October 25 away from home, so the creature might make its yearly prowl.

No one knows for sure who or what the ghostly intruder is. Speculation is that it lost its hand in an accident or crime in the Wilson House on an October night in the distant past, and that it continues to search for the missing member.

Should you happen to be driving through Mount Holly on the night of October 25, keep a lookout for an unearthly bluish light glowing from the windows of an old house. If you see it, you have found the thing that has terrified folks here since 1886.

The Dark Side
of Divinatioin

*People do not need Satan to recruit them to evil. They are
quite capable of recruiting themselves.*

M. Scott Peck

Since the mid-1960s, the practice of fortune-telling, or divination, has grown in popularity in the United States.
Whether through astrology, palm reading, consultations with
psychics or mediums, tarot cards, or Ouija boards, Americans
are fascinated with the possibility of gaining insight into the future through the interpretation of omens or by using supernatural forces.

Actually, fortune-telling is as old as humanity itself. Every
recorded culture has practiced some form of divination. Over
the centuries, the methods have varied. In ancient Greece, oracles
were used to foretell military victories and births. Monarchs in
medieval Europe maintained as a part of their court wizards and
astrologers for consultation about potential marriage partners
and political matters.

In the early part of the nineteenth century, women in Granville County employed a most unusual method of divination to catch a glimpse of their future husbands. A young lady would enter an abandoned house and remove her shimmy, or chemise. She would wash it and hang it in front of a fire to dry. When one side was completely dry, her future husband would appear, turn the shimmy, and disappear. In order for this to work, the woman had to maintain complete silence during the entire event.

This story of the macabre details the experiences of two pretty ladies who carried out this strange method of fortune-telling in a deserted Granville County house. Following the practice precisely, the women, Alice and Lola, hung their shimmies to dry and sat down to anxiously await the sight of their future spouses.

After the ladies thus invoked the powers of the supernatural, the wind began to howl and a plump black cat with glowing green eyes scampered into the house. As Alice and Lola huddled together in fear, they watched carefully to determine the significance, if any, of the cat. Their anxiety turned to delight when a small-statured man with blond hair walked in, moved directly to the roaring fireplace, turned Alice's shimmy, and promptly left. Alice had little time to ponder her fortune, because no sooner had the front door closed than it opened again. In strolled a tall man with rather dark features. Like his predecessor, he did not look at either of the ladies but rather proceeded directly to the fire. There, he pulled a knife from his pocket. Without hesitation, the man stabbed the shimmy belonging to Lola. The knife remained twisted in the undergarment as he hurried out of the house. Without saying a word to each other, the two women gathered their shimmies and raced to their respective homes. Lola stored the knife in her trunk.

As the days passed, it became evident that the fortunes of

Lola and Alice had been accurately foretold. Alice was the first to marry, and indeed, she took as her husband the blond fellow who had turned her shimmy. It took a bit longer for Lola to find her tall, dark stranger. But one Sunday, there he was at church. He was introduced to her as Jack McLenaghen. Their ensuing romance culminated in marriage.

After moving several times, Jack and Lola settled into the very house where the two girls had gone to learn their fortunes three years earlier. Although she wanted to tell him about it, Lola could never muster the courage to inform Jack of her unusual experience in the house. All the while, Jack harbored a strange feeling that he had been in the dwelling in the past.

Like most young married couples, the McLenaghens had their ups and downs. Jack was a good, kind husband except for those times, often lasting for days, when he was in a dark mood. Lola overlooked these mood swings because she loved Jack very much and did not want to anger him.

But on their third wedding anniversary, she did just that. As the couple took their seats in their buggy for the Sunday-morning ride to church, Lola remembered that she had forgotten her handkerchief. Jack volunteered to go into the house to fetch one, and Lola told him to look in her trunk. In but a moment, Jack was making his way back to the buggy. Lola could see that he was in a fit of rage. Holding up the knife, he yelled, "Where'd you get this?"

Staring at the knife as if she were looking at a ghost, Lola muttered, "Why, Jack, I don't know. I guess I found it lying around and put it there."

"I haven't seen it for four years," Jack replied, his anger mounting. Then he announced that they would forgo church in order to discuss the matter.

An hour of heated words followed. Finally, Lola related the whole story to her husband. A strange look—one that his wife had never witnessed before—came over Jack. He demanded that Lola tell him where her shimmy was. When she responded that she had given it to Alice as a keepsake, the irate husband threatened, "You were a fool to marry me knowing what would happen to you."

Tearfully and gently, Lola expressed her love for Jack. But her words were for naught, because Jack raised the knife and repeatedly slammed it into her body until she was dead. Then he casually pocketed the weapon, saddled a horse, and rode away.

Jack did not ride aimlessly. He knew exactly where he was going. His destination was Alice's home, located on the North Carolina coast. When he reached her farm, he found Alice—who by this time was a young widow—attempting to read her fortune by holding a mirror over a well.

Alice was elated when she saw reflected in the water a horse bearing a tall, dark man. But her excitement quickly turned to fear when she spied a bloody knife in his hand. From the reflection, she could not recognize that the man was Jack. Before she could turn to acknowledge him, he was gone.

Not long afterward, Jack called on Alice, who believed fate had brought him to her. In but a short time, they were married. Their lives were happy until the day a wayfarer recounted the story of an evil man who had killed his wife with a knife in Granville County, then fled to parts unknown. Alice listened intently but said nothing.

After the stranger left, Jack and Alice walked to a nearby spring to get a pail of water. She informed her husband that she knew he had murdered Lola. Jack maintained his innocence, but his face gave him away. He confessed but insisted that Alice tell him what she planned to do. She threatened to turn him in to the local sheriff. Jack would hear none of it. Out came the knife. Once again, Jack used it to do away with a wife.

When neighbors found Alice's bloody, lifeless body at the

spring the next morning, they were grieved and outraged. She had been one of the most beloved members of the community. News of her murder spread. Before nightfall, Alice McLenaghen was laid to rest and her husband, Jack, was hanging from the big oak tree at the spring.

From this twisted tale comes a word to the wise. Should you, through divination, seek to find your future mate, avoid the bizarre method of fortune-telling long ago practiced in Granville County. Otherwise, the wedding vow "for better or for worse" might take on a new, ominous meaning.

Theatrical Haunt

The unexplained things in life are more than the explained.

Oswald Chambers

The State Normal and Industrial School opened its doors on October 5, 1892, as the first state-supported school of higher education for women in North Carolina. In 1963, it made the transition to a coeducational facility. Today the beautiful, compact 180-acre campus—now the University of North Carolina at Greensboro—is home to twelve thousand students. One of the oldest and finest of the seventy-four buildings here is Aycock Auditorium, long renowned as the arts hub of the Piedmont Triad. For as long as anyone can remember, this outstanding theater building has been haunted.

To make way for the construction of the auditorium, which was completed in 1926, it was necessary to raze a house at the corner of Tate and Spring Garden Streets. That home was reputed to be haunted. According to campus tradition, it was once owned by a woman who as a young lady fell into a deep depression upon receiving the news that her fiancé had been killed in the Civil War. She never recovered from the shock. After merely existing, rather than living, for many years, she ended her sullen life by hanging herself in the attic. From the time of her death until the dwelling was taken down, her ghost resided there.

When Aycock Auditorium, an architectural masterpiece, was completed at the site of her former home, the ghost moved in. It didn't take long for her to make her presence known in the new performing-arts facility. In time, faculty and students at the university affectionately bestowed a name on the ghost—Jane Aycock—when it became apparent that she did not intend to leave. To this day, Jane continues to haunt the building, not in an evil manner but in helpful, amusing, and sometimes annoying ways.

On October 31, 1995, Lyman Collins, the auditorium manager, made a conscious effort to encounter the famed ghost. He had experienced her pranks but had never laid eyes on her. Around five o'clock that Halloween afternoon, he began the climb to the third balcony, where there had been many sightings of Jane. High above the stage, Collins took a seat in the farthest corner of the building. The auditorium was completely dark except for the glow of the light that always burned on the stage—known, ironically, as "the ghost light." After patiently waiting for the ghost, the disappointed Collins concluded that he was wasting time and decided to call it a day.

Back on the main level of the auditorium, the manager started the routine process of closing the building. As he was making his way down the hallway on the south side to check the doors, he suddenly heard a high note from a piano. Then came another and another. In a flash, he hurried into the auditorium proper. At the very moment he did so, the phantom music stopped.

Intrigued by the strange piano notes, Collins continued his investigation. He discovered that a spinet piano had been moved into an aisle by a painter. It was at that point Collins realized he had encountered the ghost. "There was no one else in the building," he recalled. "I'm certain that it was Jane, that she was telling me that the piano did not belong there. This piano was out of place, so Jane was being helpful." Collins considers her a protective spirit: "She looks out for us, and she makes sure we don't do any harm to her home."

Over the years, the theatrical phantom has been credited with turning off unnecessary lights. In fact, a switch on the auditorium lighting board is labeled "Jane's dimmer."

One student who took part in a number of campus theatrical productions in Aycock Auditorium in the 1960s noted that Jane would often announce her presence "by making the flies above the stage swing in a circular fashion, as a hanged corpse would swing." Accordingly, the ghost was considered a good-luck omen, for, as the student explained, "if the flies were swinging, we'd have a good performance; if not, well, things wouldn't go very well."

Most students and faculty members who have witnessed Jane's antics over the decades have concurred that she is a friendly, altruistic ghost. But there are some who are not so complimentary. In the late 1990s, a student, while acknowledging that Jane had never physically harmed anyone, commented, "I wouldn't say she goes out of her way to be nice and friendly. She's a prankster." And Lyman Collins admitted, "There are people that it does give the creeps to."

Although Collins didn't catch a glimpse of her that Halloween afternoon in 1995, Jane has been observed by a number of individuals—all of them men—who were working in the auditorium. For some unknown reason, the ghost has never physically manifested itself before women. Those who have seen it describe the apparition as that of a woman with gray hair and a sweet smile. It is speculated that Jane is most often sighted in the upper reaches of the auditorium because she hanged herself in the attic of her old house. But she has also been spotted in other parts of the building.

A theater major who graduated in 1999 saw Jane on one occasion and felt the touch of her hand on another. On a fall evening in 1995, he and a friend stopped at the back door of the auditorium after turning out the lights and securing the building. He described what happened next: "I looked up, and there goes Jane walking by. It was just a very fair-looking woman with light-colored hair. She walked past the window and kept on walking. We couldn't quite figure it out because we knew there was nobody in the building." During a production of *The Phantom of the Opera*, the same student descended to the basement of Aycock, where the props were stored. As he stooped to look for a needed item, he felt the eerie touch of a hand on his shoulder. He looked quickly behind him, but no one was there. As fast as he could, the young man made his way back to the stage, only to find every cast member in the same position as when he had left. Never again did he venture to the basement alone.

In September 1997 while the musical The Who's *Tommy* was being staged, a senior working on the production caught a glimpse of Jane as he began to ascend the basement steps. He explained, "I saw something in white walking up the stairway into the orchestra pit."

Jane has likewise appeared before faculty members. In 1998, while he was directing *Bye Bye Birdie*, Tom Behm, a veteran theater professor, had a frightening encounter with the ghost. Having forgotten his briefcase, he returned to Aycock to retrieve it about half-past eleven one evening. While he was standing in the middle of the dimly lit auditorium, the stage lights suddenly began to flash on and off. Then he saw her. Professor Behm later recalled, "This white kind of apparition, smoke-like thing passed across the stage and came down the steps and was walking toward me. I got out of there." His ghostly experience made a lasting impression on him: "I have never gone to Aycock by my-self again—especially late at night—because of the fear of see-ing that ghost of Jane Aycock again."

Ever since the Great Depression, historic Aycock Auditorium has served as a wonderful venue for countless theatrical and musical performances that have brought great enjoyment to pa-trons. One unseen audience member has attended every rehearsal and performance staged here. Perhaps the elderly female ghost finds contentment in the old auditorium because the gloomy house that stood at this site was transformed into a place of hap-piness and laughter, the very things that she longed for but never found in her sad, melancholy life.

Ghosts with a Scottish Accent

Ah no—round hill and plain
Wandering, he haunts, at fancy's strong command,
This spot . . .

William Wordsworth

Many colorful characters have called North Carolina home during the long history of the place named by King Charles II of England in his own honor. One of the most fascinating Tar Heels of all time was Neill "Red" MacNeill, an early settler in the Upper Cape Fear Valley. Red MacNeill gained lasting fame in the middle of the eighteenth century when he introduced barbecued meat to southeastern North Carolina. His culinary contribution is but one of his legacies. Another is his ghost, which is yet observed along the banks of the Cape Fear River in Harnett County.

In 1739, a group of three hundred settlers began the great Scottish invasion of the Cape Fear Valley, which continued for more than a quarter of a century. Included in that group was a giant of a man. Standing six foot six, Neill MacNeill was known for his beautiful red hair and curly beard. To his Scottish brethren, he was known as Neill Ruadh or *Ruadh Mon*—"the Big Red One."

An ex-sailor, Red MacNeill was by nature an adventurer and explorer. Consequently, he reconnoitered much of the river valley in search of prime parcels of land to which he could stake a claim. At his side more often than not was Archie Buie, his little bowlegged friend. Buie was a master of the bagpipes whose haunting tunes could be heard as he and Red traversed the countryside.

MacNeill had a favorite spot in the Upper Cape Fear Valley. In 1753, he purchased a sixty-acre tract on the east bank of the river near Smileys Falls. Located several miles upstream from Averasboro, Smileys Falls is a succession of rock ledges in the Cape Fear near the mouth of Upper Little Creek. At most of the ledges, the water drops only six to eighteen inches, but two falls measure four and five feet, respectively. Two of MacNeill's fellow Scottish settlers, Matthew and Nathaniel Smiley, bestowed their name on the falls when they put down roots on the east bank of the river in 1739.

Despite the beauty of his special piece of soil at Smileys Falls, Red MacNeill was possessed of a wanderlust that drove him to prepare for an expedition to the wilderness of the Yadkin River and beyond. Unfortunately, his plan never came to fruition because he was stricken during the fever epidemic of 1761. The fever was fatal to most everyone who contracted it.

Red had time to prepare for his death, thanks to his strong, massive body. He was joined at his cabin site near Smileys Falls by his ever-faithful friend, Archie Buie. Archie felled a gum tree selected by Red, then sawed a ten-foot portion of it lengthwise down the middle. While he was yet physically able to work, the red-headed Scotsman used a mallet and chisel to hew out his own coffin. To ensure a perfect fit, the dying man often lay down in the hollowed-out log. All the while, Archie's bagpipes poured out melancholy airs up and down the riverbank.

One day as Red worked to add the final touches to his coffin, the Reverend James Campbell, the famous pioneer Presbyterian minister in the Cape Fear Valley, called upon his fellow Scotsman to offer consolation and spiritual guidance. He was warmly greeted by the greatly weakened giant, but he also received an admonition: "Ye are welcome as a friend, dominie. But I want none o' yer prayers or yer religious cantin'. I ha'e ne'er called on Him when I was strong, an' I'll be damned if I go whimperin' like a coward to Him now." In a voice filled with understanding, Campbell lifted up a prayer that gave thanks for the life of one who had helped other settlers and that sought mercy for the soul of the dying man.

With each passing day, death drew closer. Finally, one evening, the end was at hand. As he labored to breathe, Red called Archie to his side and made his last request: "Bury me across the river and on the brow o' Smileys Hill where it faces west. When ye ha'e buried me, speed me on my way wi' a swirlin' o' the pipes." Then blood flowed from his dry, cracked lips, and Red MacNeill passed over to the other side.

As much as Archie wanted to honor his friend's last wish, nature would not cooperate. The rising waters of the Cape Fear rendered it impossible to move the coffin across the river to the west bank. As a result, Red's self-made casket was lowered into a grave prepared near his cabin within sight of Smileys Falls. After he shoveled the last spade of dirt on the grave, the diminutive fellow stood nearby and piped a doleful lament. The heartbroken Archie later ventured into the western wilderness of which his friend had dreamed. He was never again seen along the Cape Fear.

Not long after Red's death, numerous accounts came from

Smileys Falls of the eerie apparition of a red-headed giant standing on a rock, his arm pointing westward. Over the years, the sightings continued. Then, in the wake of General William T. Sherman's crossing of the Cape Fear in March 1865, the river again flooded. When the raging current subsided, area residents discovered that a gum-log coffin had washed ashore. Inside was the skeleton of a tall man with red hair and a red beard. Those familiar with the legend of Red MacNeill lovingly reinterred the coffin in the Smiley family cemetery on the west bank of the river in an attempt to comply with the giant's last request. Perhaps they believed that his ghost would then disappear. After all, the west bank already had its own ghost!

In 1773, Matthew Smiley, the son of Nathaniel, had been shot to death while sitting in his cabin by an unknown assailant, who opened fire from a nearby hill. To this day, the identity of the murderer remains unknown. Not long after Matthew Smiley was killed, the ghost of a gloomy man began to make its appearance on the west bank at Smileys Falls. According to eyewitnesses, it would approach them in an inquisitive manner, make an inspection, and then vanish. Most who came face to face with the apparition concluded that Matthew's ghost was relentlessly searching to find the killer.

Following the burial of Red MacNeill on the same side of the river as Matthew Smiley, two glowing apparitions have been witnessed on numerous occasions. They sometimes travel together during the night, providing eerie illumination on the otherwise dark riverbank. Could it be that the ghosts of Matthew Smiley and Red MacNeill have found pleasure in each other's company?

There is still more to the hauntings at Smileys Falls. It is said that at night, when the wind blows from the north, you can hear strange sounds faintly echoing down the river. If you listen closely, you will detect the forlorn strains of phantom bagpipes. Maybe the ghost of Archie Buie continues to serenade his beloved friend on the west bank of the Cape Fear, just as the little bowlegged Scotsman promised long ago.

The Night They Came from the Skies

*I can assure you that flying saucers, given they exist, are
not constructed by any power on earth.*

Harry Truman

From the beginning of recorded history, human beings have been captivated, mystified, and frightened by unknown
lights and objects in the heavens. In the last decade of the nineteenth
century, Americans reported seeing mysterious dirigible-shaped air-
ships with extremely bright searchlights. But on June 24, 1947, an
event occurred that sparked the American fascination with unidentified flying objects that has grown unabated since that time. On
that day, Kenneth Arnold, a businessman and pilot, spotted nine
crescent-shaped objects near his airplane as he flew above the
Cascade Mountains in Washington. When he reported that the
unusual aircraft moved "like a saucer would if you skipped it
across the water," the term *flying saucer* was born.

Long before Kenneth Arnold popularized flying saucers, unidentified flying objects were observed in the skies above North

Carolina. On August 2, 1860, William R. Killian, a forty-five-year-old minister, reported sighting a strange object that made a dangerously close approach to the earth in mountainous Jackson County. In a letter to his wife, Killian expressed the opinion that the strange object that came out of the sky might have been a comet: "Last evening about 11 o'clock there was a curious circumstance took place as I was returning from evening meeting. There was a large comet passed so near that we could plainly feel the heat in a few minutes after it passed; there were two loud cracks, one immediately after the other, and went off with a droll lumbering for several minutes, like unto hot rocks thrown into a barrel of water, which alarmed some of the families very much."

Thousands upon thousands of objects have been reported in the skies over North Carolina since the Reverend Killian recounted his sighting in the Great Smoky Mountains. Many of these UFOs have subsequently been explained as hoaxes and pranks; temperature inversions and other natural weather phenomena; planets and other celestial bodies; birds; conventional and unconventional man-made aircraft; and mirages. On the other hand, there have been sightings in the Tar Heel skies that science has been unable to explain, leading eyewitnesses and others to deem these objects to be of extraterrestrial origin. For lack of a better name, they are flying saucers.

Even more intriguing is the possibility that one of these strange, otherworldly craft has landed on North Carolina soil. If several credible eyewitness reports from southeastern North Carolina are to be believed, an alien craft set down in Hoke County in the last decade of the twentieth century. For the sake of privacy, this account will not use the actual names of those involved.

About half-past midnight on Saturday, June 27, 1992—a night of significant thunderstorm activity—Dana Melton and her mother, Jane Reynolds, were preparing to go to bed in their home, located three miles west of Raeford, the seat of Hoke County. Dana's husband and young son had already retired. Suddenly, the two women were startled by a loud roar reminiscent of a freight train. It caused the entire house to vibrate. Fearful that bad weather—perhaps even a tornado—was striking the area, they stood motionless until the commotion stopped. Rushing to the windows, Dana and Jane peered out. They noticed that their outdoor security light and that of their neighbor had been extinguished. But in the darkness, they could see it—an object approximately the size of a swimming pool was either resting on or hovering over a hayfield 150 feet away. Even though they could not ascertain the overall nature of the craft, the curved nature of the reddish orange windows around the bottom led the women to believe that it was dome-shaped. No noise could be heard. It was difficult to determine whether the object had actually landed.

Dana recounted her first impressions of the craft: "It looked like a fire burning in the woods, but the more you looked at it, it was like orange windows around it. It was like it was just sitting there looking at us, and we were looking at it. And it was quiet."

Sprawling Fort Bragg—the home of the Eighty-second Airborne, Special Forces, Delta Team, and Pope Air Force Base—is located just six miles from the Melton residence. Dana surmised that perhaps a military aircraft had crashed. She was mindful that United States Air Force A-100s flew over the area on a frequent basis. As a result, she promptly called the Hoke County Sheriff's Department and related the incident. She was told that help was on the way.

While she waited, curiosity got the best of her. Dana and her mother turned on the porch light and bravely ventured to the front of the house to get a better view of the eerie object. As soon as they stepped outside, the UFO went dark and vanished into the cloudy night skies. As it disappeared, the outdoor lights came back on.

A few minutes later, six squad cars drove up to the Melton residence. Out stepped a dozen deputies. Although none of the officers had seen the object, several had heard its roar when it passed them. After the two eyewitnesses were questioned, the sheriff's department prepared an official report on the incident. It stated that Dana and her mother were not under the influence of alcohol or narcotics. When the deputies contacted Fort Bragg, base officials indicated that all aircraft had been grounded that night as a result of the bad weather.

The day after they sighted the UFO, Dana and Jane walked over to the field where they had observed the strange craft. There, they saw an area of swirled grass measuring fifteen feet in diameter. There were two bare spots in the center of the circle.

Two weeks later, a representative of a national organization established to investigate UFO sightings visited the site. He reported that it had the appearance of a classic "saucer nest."

Something came out of the sky and touched the Hoke County landscape in the wee hours of the morning on Saturday, June 27, 1992. Was it one of Kenneth Arnold's so-called flying saucers? You be the judge.

A Bridge to the Supernatural

Listen to their marvelous tales of ghosts and goblins, and haunted fields, and haunted brooks, and haunted bridges.

Washington Irving

Bridges are among the most common places where ghosts and other supernatural creatures are encountered. No one is exactly sure why this is so, but it is most likely because bridges are by their nature dangerous places where tragic deaths frequently occur. Iredell County has two of the most famous haunted bridges in all of North Carolina.

Bostian's Bridge is a railroad span just west of Statesville, the county seat. On August 27, 1891, a passenger train bound from Salisbury to Asheville derailed and plunged off Bostian's Bridge into a deep ravine, killing thirty people. Ever since that time, at precisely 3:00 A.M. on each anniversary of the wreck, a ghostly repetition of the disaster has occurred. People living near the site have heard the phantom sounds of human screams, crashing metal, and the rupturing of steam pipes.

Although Bostian's Bridge is far better known in the ghostly lore of the Tar Heel State, the Warren Bridge, a highway span, has an even more frightening story associated with it. Located on SR 1807 (Warrens Bridge Road) nearly three miles northwest of Union Grove, the existing Warren Bridge is a modern concrete structure that crosses Hunting Creek near the Wilkes County line. It was constructed to replace the wooden bridge that was in service when a grisly murder took place nearby on June 15, 1916. Though the Warren Bridge has changed in appearance and sophistication over the years, one thing has remained constant: the terrifying screams heard ever since Claude A. Warren met his untimely death nearby in the second decade of the twentieth century. Indeed, the bridge memorializes the name of the man whose ghost may now roam here.

Claude Warren was a farmer who shared a tract of land along Hunting Creek with his brother-in-law, Homer Matheson. By the late spring of 1916, there was bad blood between the two men. Rumor had it that the hostility began when Warren turned Matheson in for operating a liquor still on the creek. But Matheson told authorities that his brother-in-law had initiated the feud by threatening to kill Matheson over an insignificant matter.

Whatever the cause of the disagreement, matters reached a boiling point after Warren reported Matheson for practicing deception and fraud in his business. The trouble came about one day as Matheson was loading a wagon with cotton to take to the gin to be weighed. Warren watched as his wife's brother buried an anvil deep under the cotton to add to the weight. Upon learning that his own brother-in-law had snitched on him, Matheson was outraged.

It was in the late afternoon of that fateful day in early June 1916 when the squabble turned deadly. On hand to witness the heated altercation was Mary Matheson, the wife of Homer and the sister of Claude. As the words and threats grew in intensity, Mary pleaded with her loved ones to calm down and make peace. But her adjurations seemed to have no effect until her brother turned to walk away. As he did, Homer Matheson picked up his loaded shotgun, pulled the trigger, and sent forth a well-aimed shell that exploded in the back of Warren's head. Mary unleashed a bloodcurdling scream as her mortally wounded brother fell to the ground.

Ultimately, her husband confessed to the murder and was brought to justice. But the frightful screams did not end. Close to dark every afternoon following the murder, phantom screams pierced the stillness along the creek.

In a short time, the Warren Bridge came to be recognized by area residents as a haunted place. Children were warned by their parents to avoid it because of the ghosts that were said to lurk nearby. Most obliged and refused to cross the span, particularly after dark.

The afternoon screams heard to this day at the bridge are said to be those of the ghost of Mary Matheson. As to the identity of the other ghosts, no one is quite sure. Some people believe that one of them represents the headless Claude Warren, who continues the relentless search for his head, blown away by the shotgun blast.

If a pleasant afternoon drive in the Brushy Mountains of Wilkes County and northern Iredell County should take you across the Warren Bridge, listen carefully for a shrill sound. Be advised that it is not the wind. Rather, it is the ghostly lament of a lady who saw the lives of her brother and husband destroyed in a fleeting moment almost a century ago.

The Spirit(ed) Battle Rages On

*On great fields something stays. Forms change and pass;
bodies disappear; but spirits linger, to consecrate ground for the
vision-place of souls.*

General Joshua Lawrence Chamberlain

As a stalwart supporter of the fight for American
independence and in the subsequent struggle for Southern independence, North Carolina was fortunate that it did not serve as
a major battleground in either of the two largest wars fought in
the United States. Be that as it may, the battle long considered
by many historians as the last grand stand of the Confederacy
was waged in Johnston County beginning on March 19, 1865.
When the three days of fighting were over, the Battle of
Bentonville stood as the bloodiest battle ever fought on North
Carolina soil, a dubious distinction that it holds to this day.

There are some who maintain that the battle is yet being
fought. Over the past hundred years or so, numerous visitors to
the site have come away with eyewitness accounts of the military activities of two phantom armies of the nineteenth century.

Following the Federal capture of Fort Fisher and the port of Wilmington on the North Carolina coast during the first two months of 1865, General William T. Sherman pushed his pair of thirty-thousand-man columns north into the Tar Heel State in the first week of March. His massive army, greatly fatigued from the campaign in Georgia and South Carolina, was anxious to reach Goldsboro, where a train waited with badly needed supplies.

While the Union troops were crossing into the Sandhills region of North Carolina, General Joseph E. Johnston, the Virginian who had recently accepted the daunting task of stopping Sherman before he could unite with the army of General U. S. Grant, was desperate to find a strategic place where his outnumbered army could do battle with the Yankees. Johnston's outstanding cavalry chieftain, General Wade Hampton, located an excellent site near Bentonville, a small village on the road to Goldsboro, which was twenty miles to the east.

Sunday, March 19, broke clear and beautiful as Johnston's ragtag twenty-thousand-man army positioned itself for an ambush. From every part of the South—from as far north as Maryland as far west and south as Texas—they had come to make a gallant effort to halt the ever-growing Yankee momentum. Shoulder to shoulder in battle formation, gray-bearded grandfathers stood with Tar Heel teenagers who had never pressed a razor to their faces. About midmorning, the left column of Sherman's army marched headlong into the waiting Confederate rifles. For three days, a fierce battle raged as the beleaguered and outmanned Confederates heroically stood their ground.

When it was all over on March 21, neither side could claim a battlefield victory. Nonetheless, Sherman got what he wanted: he was able to push forward to Goldsboro. Less than three weeks after the clash at Bentonville, the Civil War, for all intents and purposes, ended with Lee's surrender to Grant at Appomattox.

The casualties at Bentonville were enormous. Confederate

losses were listed at 2,606, while Union totals were set at 1,527. Many of the wounded and dying from both armies received medical attention at the Harper House, a two-story farmhouse located on the battleground. Amputated limbs were tossed from open windows as army surgeons went about their grim duties. Screams of pain filled the dwelling, and blood flowed on the wooden floors.

In the days following the battle, things returned to normal at Bentonville. The Harper family reclaimed its house. Crops sprang forth from the grounds that months earlier had served as the killing fields of the dying Confederacy. But ultimately, the Harpers decided to vacate their house. Perhaps they already knew what later visitors to the dwelling would learn—the house was haunted by the spirits of the battle's victims. After the Harpers left, the house remained devoid of human occupants. Local folks refused to go near the place after the sun went down, as terrible moans and groans could be heard emanating from it.

Exactly forty years after the Battle of Bentonville officially ended, the first of many eyewitness accounts of the battles between two ghostly Civil War armies was recorded. Close to midnight on a Saturday in March 1905, Jim Weaver, a thirty-six-year-old Bentonville farmer, was scouting the pine forest where a portion of the battle had been fought. That dark night in rural southern Johnston County, Weaver had in his company Joseph Lewis, a young Englishman who was intent upon learning the art of hunting. When Red, Weaver's trusted coon dog, treed its prey, his master grabbed an ax to take down the pine where the coon was hiding. At the very moment he delivered the first blow to the tree, a brilliant white light flashed nearby. Before either of the stunned men could react, a second, third, and fourth flash intervened. Suddenly, the entire forest was illuminated with countless bursts of light. The men were astonished at what they then saw—soldiers in blue Civil War uniforms running in the distance. Then came the sounds of gunfire, human screams, and all the other noises associated with battle. Galloping horses mounted by gray-clad soldiers sped past the bewildered hunters. As guns blazed and men fell wounded around them, there was no doubt about it—a Civil War battle was being fought!

At the height of the supernatural clash, the attention of the two observers was drawn to the action near the pine tree where they stood. A young Confederate flag-bearer was engaged in desperate hand-to-hand combat with a Yankee. When another Southern soldier, older than his comrade, attempted to intervene, the Federal soldier shot him in the heart. Then the Northerner drew his knife, thrust it into the left shoulder of his young adversary, grabbed his flag, and raced away into the ongoing fight.

With bullets, whether phantom or real, whizzing about their heads, Jim Weaver and Joseph Lewis realized that their personal safety was at issue. They ran out of the woods and into the field on a route that took them past the long-deserted Harper House. There, they received yet another shock. In the windows of the old dwelling, they could see strange lights and fiery ghosts.

The following morning, Jim Weaver was only too happy to attend Sunday worship services after his brush with the paranormal. Indeed, he was anxious to relate his extraordinary tale to a group of friends at church. Among the men assembled to listen was a fifty-seven-year-old Confederate veteran with a crippled left arm. At the conclusion of Jim's story, the old soldier spoke with great emotion: "Forty years ago today, me and my oldest brother was at the Battle of Bentonville. I was just a boy at the time, so they had me carrying the flag." Nodding toward his withered arm, the soft-spoken man said this: "I lost that flag to a Yankee soldier, who gave me this instead. My brother got killed trying to save me and that Rebel flag."

Today, a sizable portion of the Civil War battlefield, including the restored Harper House, is preserved as Bentonville

Battleground State Historic Site. Located on the grounds are a number of monuments and a visitor center. Among the artifacts at the site is the flag of the Fortieth North Carolina, which was captured by the Fourteenth Michigan. It was this flag that was taken from the young soldier in the drama replayed in 1905 before the eyes of Jim Weaver and Joseph Lewis.

Each year, thousands of visitors and reenactors make their way to the historic site. Many leave firmly convinced that the Harper House and the adjacent battlefield are haunted. For example, while a site employee was conducting a tour of the house for a group from Manassas, Virginia, one of the tourists sensed the presence of ghosts. She exclaimed, "Well, there's one of the family now. I can see him."

Confused by the comment, the employee asked, "What do you see?"

The lady proceeded to describe a man standing nearby that the others could not see: "He is very tall and has a white beard, but no mustache. He is wearing a long black coat and has very, very thick, dark eyebrows." According to the woman, the man was "looking very intently down into the yard." Suddenly, he turned and looked at her.

The woman had never seen a picture of Mr. Harper, the master of the house at the time of the war, but her description of him was nothing less than perfect.

As the tour of the house progressed, the lady continued to speak of the ghostly sights she observed. Her accounts coincided with actual events that had taken place. She saw ambulance wagons pull up to the house. One of the wounded soldiers she saw being treated in the house was a Union general. At that point, John Goode, the site coordinator, discounted her revelations, since he had never heard of a general officer being wounded in the battle. Not long after the tour, however, a visitor from Ohio called at the site. In the course of his tour, the man remarked that his great-grandfather, General Benjamin D. Fearing, had been treated for his battle wounds in the Harper House. He had the papers to prove it. As a commander of the Fourteenth Corps, General Fearing had played a prominent role in the battle. The Harper House had served as the field hospital for that corps.

Visitors to the house have reported the odd sensation that they were being watched. Others have felt the icy touch of phantom hands.

Some men who were would-be thieves also experienced the ghosts of the Harper House. After turning themselves in to the authorities, the men confessed that as soon as they broke into the building, they felt an unusual chill. Then they heard heavy footsteps pacing back and forth on the second floor. When it sounded as if someone was coming down the steps, one of the criminals pointed his flashlight in that direction. There stood the angry apparition of Mr. Harper. The men promptly scampered out the open front door, which mysteriously slammed behind them.

Even site employees have encountered the supernatural at the Harper House. One man was working alone in the dwelling on a chilly, rainy morning. Upon hearing a strange noise upstairs, he checked each room but found nothing. After returning to the first floor, he could not shake the feeling that someone was in the house with him. He looked up the staircase and saw a ghostly figure standing at the top of the steps. Terrified, he abandoned his post and ran to the safety of the visitor center.

Local people have also had supernatural encounters with the Harper family. One evening about twilight, a Johnston County man visited the Harper family cemetery, which is located near the mass grave where more than 750 Confederate battle dead were laid to rest. After inspecting the graveyard, the man opened his car door and climbed back into the vehicle. With the interior light glowing, he looked into his rearview mirror. To his horror, there was an old lady sitting in the backseat. According to the visitor, the woman's hair was "pulled back in a bun, and she had on a high-neck, black dress." It is believed that the man saw the apparition of Mrs. Amy Harper. So frightened was he that he slammed the accelerator to the floor and sped away. When he finally mustered the nerve to look behind him again, the backseat was empty.

Frequent encounters with the supernatural in the adjacent fields and forests seem to suggest that a ghostly Civil War battle is still under way here. While visiting the Confederate mass grave in 1989, a Durham police officer could hear the rhythmic *tap-tap-tap* of drums, as if an army were marching into battle on the east side of the field. Then the same steady *tap-tap-tap* began on the west side of the field. On that day, there were no reenactors or bands present.

Some of the earthworks from the 1865 battle have been preserved at the historic site. At these crude fortifications, loud booms have been heard from time to time. People who have experienced the sensation likened the sound to artillery blasts. Strangely, the ground shook with the mysterious detonations. On each occasion, there was no local storm activity.

Although artifact hunting is strictly prohibited on the battleground, treasure hounds have come under the cloak of night to scour the site for remnants of the battle. For most of these plunderers, one nighttime foray into the supernatural has proven to be all they could stand. One such group foraging in the forest was terrified by the sudden appearance of flickering lights all about, as old candle lanterns held by ghostly hands swung to and fro. And more than one scavenger has run away in abject fear after hearing phantom rifles being cocked.

And what about the bizarre battle that Jim Weaver and Joseph Lewis witnessed in the first decade of the twentieth century? Is it still being fought? If Civil War reenactors are to be believed, the Battle of Bentonville never ended.

Following the centennial observance of the Civil War from 1961 to 1965, reenacting has steadily grown in popularity throughout America. Reenactors, both men and women, take their hobby very seriously. Every year during the anniversary of the battle, hundreds of these weekend warriors descend on Bentonville to take part in the reenactment of the horrific engagement.

From time to time, reenactors from both armies conduct a nighttime skirmish in the woods of the battlefield. Site personnel have watched balls of light flash up and down the lines as the authentic weapons were fired. And then, in the distance along the bottom of the tree line, they have witnessed similar lights, as if another group of soldiers was discharging its weapons. But no reenactors were there!

Not long after the annual reenactments at Bentonville began, two historic-site guards were directing the arriving reenactors to their respective camps in the wee hours of the morning. A heavy fog lay over the battleground. As the two men chatted, they began to hear approaching footsteps. Site coordinator John Goode described what happened next: "It sounded like a fairly sizable group of people. Pretty soon, they could see their forms coming down the road toward them. It was a group of what they assumed to be reenactors dressed as Union infantry. There were about a hundred of them."

When the soldiers came into full view, the guards were highly impressed with the authenticity of their uniforms. "One of the first things the guards noticed was that their uniforms were just absolutely ragged, which is one thing we've always known about Sherman's army," Goode said. "They had been out of supplies for over a month and campaigning in a territory like this, so it had a very bad effect on their uniforms. These guys marched up to the guards and turned, going back toward the Union camp.

They were in perfect step. Nobody said a thing. They were lean-looking, and you could hear the tin canteens and cups clanking as they marched past."

Later that morning, after all the reenactors had arrived for the planned events, the two guards strolled over to the Union encampment to compliment the men on their historic-looking costumes. To their dismay, they found only thirty to forty soldiers present. When they inquired about the large contingent of Union soldiers that had marched past them earlier, the bewildered reenactors could not offer a clue.

Owned and operated by the state of North Carolina, Bentonville Battleground State Historic Site is located several miles west of US 701 on SR 1008. No admission is charged to tour the place where the last significant hopes of the Confederacy died in 1865. But should you pay a visit, beware that the last great showdown of the Civil War may not yet be over. Indeed, the ghostly soldiers at Bentonville continue to play out one of the most haunting chapters in all of American history.

The Sins of the Father

The belief in a supernatural source of evil is not necessary;
men alone are quite capable of every wickedness.

Joseph Conrad

Historians generally agree that the Revolutionary War in North Carolina was at times little more than a civil war in which Tar Heels, both soldiers and civilians, resorted to barbarism and cruelty the likes of which the state has never witnessed since. There is little dispute that the most infamous of the Tories who dispensed mayhem and violence in North Carolina during that time was David Fanning. So egregious were his wartime activities that Fanning was one of only three Tories the state legislature refused to pardon in 1783.

Fanning used the Deep River area as the staging ground for his heinous partisan activities. His choice was a bit ironic, since his father had drowned in the river just before David's birth. From the northeastern edge of Moore County, the Deep River flows north to form the dividing line between Chatham and Lee Counties and ultimately joins the Haw River to form the mighty Cape Fear. It was in this area that one of the strangest births in North Carolina history occurred as the Revolutionary War drew to a close.

After the British abandoned North Carolina in November 1781, many of Fanning's civilian soldiers began to flee in fear of reprisals by the victorious Patriots. One such evacuee was Captain William Lindley, who resided in Chatham County. Lindley, a commander of a local force of Tories, was well liked by his Patriot neighbors because he conducted himself in a gentlemanly, civilized manner. But despite his excellent reputation, Captain Lindley reasoned that he would not be safe at home until anti-British sentiment subsided. Accordingly, Lindley, one of Fanning's dearest friends, set out for the relative safety of the Watauga settlement on the other side of the Blue Ridge in what is now Tennessee.

Unbeknownst to Lindley, two of his comrades in arms were hot on his trail. These men, William White and John Magaharty, had an unknown grievance against the Tory officer. They overtook him near the New River. A violent confrontation ensued. Lindley's assailants were delighted to find their prey unarmed. When they drew their swords, the officer raised his hands in a futile effort to deflect the sharp blades. White and Magaharty attacked with savage force. Lindley's fingers were severed, and one of the swords lodged in his skull. The murderers were not satiated until they had thoroughly mutilated the corpse.

Upon their return to the Deep River area, the two men boasted of their exploits. When David Fanning learned that two of his own men had slain his unarmed confidant, he was outraged. He sent forth his men to hunt down White and Magaharty and bring them to him. At length, the two unfortunate fellows were delivered to Fanning, who promptly meted out his special form of justice. They were hanged to death on the same limb of a large, stately tree near the Tory camp.

In the wake of the executions, David Fanning paid a personal visit to the pregnant wife of William White, who is believed to have lived along the Deep River in what is now Lee County. There, Fanning took great delight in announcing the hanging death of the unborn child's father. Then he related to the weeping widow every gory detail of her husband's gruesome attack on Captain Lindley. By the time Fanning departed, the poor woman was in shock.

Fanning later fled to Canada, where he lived out the rest of his long life.

Mrs. White gave birth to a son. Even though the child bore some likeness to his deceased father, he more resembled the slain Captain Lindley, for, you see, the poor boy was born without several fingers on one hand and with a strange and rather unsightly birthmark on his head. These defects and blemishes matched exactly the fatal blows inflicted upon Captain Lindley by the child's father just months earlier.

Malvina of Woodside

Now there is nothing but the ghosts of things—
No life, no love, no children, and no men.

Edwin Arlington Robinson

Nestled in the rolling foothills of North Carolina, venerable Lincolnton is the state's second-oldest incorporated town west of the Catawba River. Chartered by the state legislature in 1785, the city was the birthplace of the Southern textile industry and the site of a significant Revolutionary War battle. A number of historic homes, reminders of Lincolnton's proud past, are located throughout the city and the adjacent countryside.

One such home is Woodside, a magnificent late-eighteenth-century Federal-style brick plantation house on NC 182 approximately two miles west of Lincolnton. Erected in 1799, the well-preserved masterpiece survives as the third-oldest house in Lincoln County.

As important as its architectural significance are the prominent persons who have called Woodside home. Lawson Henderson, the original owner, was a wealthy planter who amassed an estate that exceeded two thousand acres. Henderson was also a political powerhouse who served as clerk of superior court for thirty years and then boldly declared the office his for life. One of his sons born at Woodside, James Pinckney Henderson (1808-1858), was destined for political greatness in a faraway place. As an adult, James migrated to Texas, where he emerged with his friends Sam Houston and Stephen Austin as the great heroes of the fight for independence from Mexico. Subsequently, he served as the European ambassador for the Republic of Texas. In 1846, he was elected the first governor of the state of Texas.

Two years later, James Pinckney Henderson's widowed mother sold Woodside to Dr. Alexander Ramseur. In 1858, Ramseur's daughter, Alice, married a local physician, John Richardson. The newlyweds made their home at Woodside. Among the five children born to the Richardsons at the plantation was Malvina, a beautiful daughter.

In the aftermath of the Civil War, Woodside fared as did many other plantations in North Carolina and throughout the South. Although the mansion was spared the torch of General George Stoneman and his Yankee raiders when they arrived in Lincolnton on April 30, 1865, the plantation economy was forever at an end. As a result, the Richardson family was forced to find an alternate means of income to keep the estate viable.

During Reconstruction, wealthy Northerners began making extended hunting trips to the Lincolnton area. Dr. Richardson quartered some of the hunters in the mansion and allowed them to hunt pheasant on the estate grounds. Meanwhile, Malvina had matured into a beautiful young woman who busied herself as a teacher at the school conducted for local children at Woodside.

One of the visiting hunters who enjoyed the hospitality in

Dr. Richardson's fine home was young and strikingly handsome. His name has long been lost to history, but he will be called Jim for the purposes of this story. Early into his visit at Woodside, Jim met Malvina. Theirs was love at first sight. Jim soon asked Dr. Richardson for Malvina's hand in marriage. Assured by Malvina that she was deeply in love with Jim, the physician graciously consented.

The couple made plans for a spectacular wedding at Woodside. An exquisite gown was sewn for the bride, who was to descend the mansion's grand staircase during the ceremony.

But as the big day neared, the cruel hand of fate dealt the couple a tragic blow. Jim was suddenly stricken with fever. Despite Dr. Richardson's valiant efforts to save his life, the young man died after a short illness. Because Jim's parents were traveling in Europe at the time, a grave was prepared in the cemetery located near Woodside. However, before Jim's body could be buried there, a telegram arrived at the plantation. The Richardsons agreed to comply with the request contained therein: the body was to be returned to Jim's home in the North.

When the disconsolate Malvina learned that her beloved Jim was to be interred in a land so distant, she asked that her family accompany her on a walk to the plantation cemetery. At the burial site prepared for Jim, she cried out in anguish, "Leave the grave open!" Her request was granted.

In but a few days, death paid another visit to Woodside. This time, it came calling for Malvina. Although the exact cause of her death was never determined, those who knew her best said that she died of a broken heart.

Following the funeral, family and friends gathered at the grave previously meant for Jim. After a solemn, tearful grave-side ceremony, they placed the coffin bearing the lovely Malvina, dressed in her wedding gown, into the ground.

A stone marks Malvina's grave. But is this her final resting place? Soon after her death, a gentleman calling at Woodside happened to peer into a side window after he had knocked at the front door. To his astonishment, he saw the apparition of a lady attired in a wedding gown floating down the grand staircase. From the description provided by the man, the ghost could have been none other than Malvina.

Over the many decades that have passed since Malvina's death, her apparition has occasionally been observed descending the grand staircase at Woodside. Perhaps she is still rehearsing the wedding that can and never will be.

Haunted Chambers

In the realm of science, all attempts to find any evidence of supernatural beings . . . have thus far failed.

David Hume

When a building is deemed haunted, it is generally assumed that it houses the spirit of a deceased person or animal. The haunting is perceived to be the result of the activities or presence of the entity from the other world. History, however, has recorded that there are objects, including buildings, that are considered to be haunted without the existence of the ghost of a former living being. These rare cases of haunted nonliving objects present some of the most bewildering enigmas of the paranormal.

One interesting example of this eerie phenomenon is found on the campus of historic Davidson College in northwestern Mecklenburg County. Founded by the Presbyterian Church in 1837, Davidson has long been regarded as an institution of academic excellence. Over its long history, the small college has produced many graduates who have distinguished themselves in various fields of human endeavor. Former Davidson students include President Woodrow Wilson and Dean Rusk, United States secretary of state during the Kennedy and Johnson administrations.

Bordering Main Street in the charming village of Davidson, the picturesque 450-acre campus contains seventy-five academic and residential buildings. Of all the structures, the most imposing is the Chambers Building. This architectural gem, completed in 1929, serves as the main academic building at the college. Designed to resemble Thomas Jefferson's Monticello, the handsome brick structure looks out over an expansive green lawn where its predecessor, Old Chambers, stood until it was gutted by fire in 1921. Campus tradition has it that the ghost of Old Chambers still lingers at its former site. From time to time, that ghost even makes a bizarre appearance to check on its offspring, much like a concerned mother.

When periods of dry weather strike the North Carolina Piedmont, students, faculty, and townspeople look for the return of the phantom building. And sure enough, a mammoth, ghost-like floor plan of Old Chambers—complete with forty-five-foot-tall columns—materializes on the sprawling lawn in front of the replacement building. Not until several drenching rains have fallen does the apparitional structure vanish.

It is little wonder that the ghost of Old Chambers haunts this campus, given the spirited history of the building. Construction of the brick edifice commenced in 1858. Funds for the project were provided from the estate of Maxwell Chambers, a wealthy cotton merchant from Salisbury. When it was completed in 1860, Old Chambers was acclaimed by some to be the greatest college building in all of America. More than twenty years after it was consumed by fire, a noted architectural historian called Old Chambers "one of the stateliest college buildings in the South, if not the entire nation."

But it was not its size or architectural elegance that made Old Chambers the most cherished landmark on the campus. When it opened its doors, Old Chambers represented a new beginning for Davidson; it stood as the proud symbol of the future of the college; and its stately presence fueled a great fire of enthusiasm on the campus.

That fire was quelled when the Civil War robbed Davidson of its students and resources. Leland Park, the director of the college library, once opined, "If it hadn't been for the Civil War, Princeton would have been known as the Davidson of the North."

Despite the great setback for Southern colleges wrought by the war, Old Chambers was the very spirit, the heart and soul, of Davidson from its birth until its fiery death more than sixty years later. Oh, the strange, eerie stories its ghost could tell!

During the last decade of the nineteenth century and the first decade of the twentieth, the now-defunct North Carolina Medical College was housed in a building adjacent to the Davidson campus. Many young men, anxious to complete their liberal-arts and medical studies as soon as possible, attended both institutions at the same time. In their course of study at the medical college, students were often required to provide corpses for their own use in the dissecting room. Consequently, it was not unusual for them to raid area cemeteries for fresh cadavers.

One such raiding party left Davidson about eight o'clock one evening for the four-hour carriage ride to Charlotte. About midnight, the students went about opening a freshly dug, unmarked grave and hauling out the coffin. Pulling from it the body of an unknown woman, the students, in their haste to leave, did little to cover the site of their misdeed. Instead, they hurriedly placed the corpse and their tools in the carriage and repaired to Davidson.

Not long after the sun dawned on the new day, workers arriving at the Charlotte cemetery noticed that someone had tampered with a grave. Upon closer inspection, they discovered that a body had been removed. As it turned out, the pilfered corpse was that of a prominent Charlotte lady. Cognizant that the North Carolina Medical College was in constant need of bodies of the recently diseased, a delegation decided to visit Davidson to examine the cadavers there.

When the students learned of the impending visit by the authorities, they decided to hide the evidence of their crime. Fortunately for the culprits, the investigators postponed their trip for a day or so. That delay provided the young men with just the window of opportunity they needed. Under cover of night, they transported the cadaver from the morgue to Old Chambers and buried it at the base of one of the large columns. Whether the corpse was removed before the columns were taken down in 1929 is unknown.

Perhaps the most famous person to live in Old Chambers was Tommy Wilson, who later became president of the United States. As a freshman at Davidson in 1873, Wilson was assigned to Room 13 on the first floor of the north wing. President Woodrow Wilson stopped by his old room when he and Mrs. Wilson visited the campus in 1916. Five years later, the college community watched in horror as a devastating fire spread quickly through Old Chambers and reduced it to rubble. Only the massive pillars remained standing. Eyewitnesses noted that the very last part of the structure to be enveloped by flames was Room 13. Following the completion of the existing Chambers Building, the four mammoth columns of its predecessor—one of them perhaps hiding a human skeleton—were taken down.

Today, the ghost of Old Chambers continues to make itself visible on occasion. Skeptics who have seen the phantom floor plan on the lawn claim that it is nothing more than the old foundation of the building, which was never removed but only covered with earth. They contend that hot, dry weather causes the grass at the site to either die or turn brown, thereby allowing the old foundation to appear.

But most people who have observed the outline of Old Chambers in the shadow of the existing structure are not so sure. Perhaps the scientific explanation is valid. Maybe, however, Old Chambers did in fact instill a new spirit at the college, a spirit that still abides at old Davidson.

The Witch of Tuckertown

I have sworn thee fair, and thought thee bright,
Who art as black as hell, as dark as night.

William Shakespeare

Tuckertown, a former mill village in northwestern Montgomery County, is now but a place name on antiquated state maps. It is not even a ghost town, because the site of the once-thriving community was flooded in 1962 when Carolina Aluminum Company built Tuckertown Lake on the Yadkin River. But before the village met its watery demise, it had a true-to-life witch.

Tuckertown was named around 1900 in honor of an official of a Northern company that opened a rope manufacturing plant along the Yadkin. Numerous dwellings were constructed in the village to house the workers at the mill.

Before World War II, an old hag by the name of Ann Blackhand lived in the community. Old Ann, as she was called by Tuckertown residents, was known to have supernatural powers. She could cast spells on human beings as well as on animals.

After the marriages of several seemingly devoted couples broke up, rumors spread that the marital discord was the evil work of Old Ann, the witch of Tuckertown. Suspicion of the old woman turned to actual fear.

On one occasion, Old Ann paid a visit to unsuspecting neighbors at their home in the village. A young woman in the house recounted the visit: "Old Ann came to our house. She gave a sweet-smelling melon of some kind to my brother. She remained at our house for a few minutes." As soon as the old woman departed, the boy experienced terrible pains. "He screamed and kicked and appeared to be on the verge of going into convulsions," his sister reported. Because the youngster had never been ill a day in his life, his mother and siblings were greatly alarmed. A friendly neighbor was summoned to render assistance. En route to the home, she noticed Ann Blackhand leaving. The neighbor promptly asked the concerned family members, "Did Old Ann give that baby anything?" The frantic mother handed the melon to her friend. It was immediately thrown into the fireplace, where it was reduced to ashes in a matter of seconds. In an instant, the afflicted child was relieved of all pain.

Old Ann's reign of terror continued. One particular Tuckertown farmer maintained a superior herd of cows that enabled him to supply the dairy needs of the villagers. Suddenly, his milch cows began to dry up. Perplexed by the problem, the farmer gave the animals more food, to no avail. At his wit's end, he poured out his worries to a friend. The neighbor recalled seeing Ann Blackhand prowling the dairy farm several weeks before. Intrigued by the revelation, the farmer hurried home, where, to his amazement, he found an unusual row of wooden pegs driven into the ground some six inches apart in an area where his animals normally grazed. He pulled up the pegs, and his cows once again produced bounteous quantities of milk.

As one hot June afternoon melted into evening, thick, dark

clouds gathered in the sky over Tuckertown. That night was one of the darkest in the memory of the mill workers. All of a sudden, the stillness was broken by a series of bloodcurdling screams coming from the home of Ann Blackhand. One villager who heard them said, "It sounded like the wail of a lost soul."

A group of daring neighbor women made haste to Old Ann's two-story house in an attempt to determine the source of the screams. Upon entering her upstairs bedroom, the fearless women discovered the witch on her bed seemingly in the throes of death. As one of the neighbors put it, "She went into cramps and was almost in a knot."

Then even stranger things began to happen. First, a chair turned over in the dark room adjacent to Old Ann's bedroom. Next, a big, black ball about the size of a wash pot came rolling out of that room and bumped heavily down the stairs. One villager, a man who settled in nearby New London after Tuckertown was flooded, dodged the fast-moving ball as it made its way out into the darkness of the village streets.

To the pleasant surprise of everyone in the village, Old Ann was instantly relieved of her pain and the mysterious evil that had caused her to become the witch of Tuckertown. Thereafter, she lived a normal life.

Ann Blackhand and all of the people who witnessed the bizarre events of that June night are dead. Before Tuckertown was flooded, most of the houses there were dismantled or moved elsewhere. Now, the site of the village lies under forty feet of water. Maybe it is best that the deep, dark secrets of Tuckertown's past remain in the depths of a watery grave.

For Whom Doth the Bell Toll?

Any man's death diminishes me, because I am involved in mankind; and therefore never send to know for whom the bell tolls . . .

John Donne

Located in southern Moore County, Aberdeen is named for the seaport of the same name in Scotland. Although the picturesque town was not incorporated until 1893, it was settled more than a century earlier, primarily by people of Scottish descent. Evidence of their early presence can be found at Old Bethesda Presbyterian Church and Cemetery on the outskirts of town.

After Old Bethesda was organized in 1790, the congregation promptly went to work and completed a sanctuary the same year. The existing white frame edifice, surmounted by a tower and spire, was erected in 1850. Of particular interest is the old church bell, which pealed a ghostly toll during the summer of 1863. That mysterious occurrence was the denouement of a beautiful love story set during the Civil War.

Like many of the residents of Aberdeen in the mid-nineteenth century, Leona Burns and Johnny Blue were Presbyterians who firmly believed in the doctrine of predestination. And if there were ever a young man and young woman predestined to be together, it had to be Leona and Johnny. Born just a year apart, the two had been almost constant companions since childhood. As they grew into teenagers, their infatuation with each other—their puppy love—grew into a serious romance.

On a beautiful, warm afternoon in the early spring of 1861, Johnny, then seventeen, sat close to sixteen-year-old Leona on the plush, green grass in the shadow of the spire of Old Bethesda. There, Johnny pledged his eternal love to Leona before he broke the doleful news to her. He was going away. Most of the states of the South had already banded together as a nation to fight the United States. It was only a matter of time until North Carolina joined this confederacy. Every able-bodied male who could shoulder a weapon was needed to go to the aid of North Carolina's Southern neighbors and to protect the borders of the Tar Heel State. Johnny was ready to take his place in the ranks of North Carolinians rallying to the cause.

Although Leona was proud of Johnny's willingness to do his duty, she could not mask her sadness and concern. Tears streamed down her cheeks as she told Johnny of her great love for him. And then she asked him to promise that he would come back home to her. In a soothing, reassuring voice, Johnny did so. But suddenly, his face took on a somber, melancholy look. As he nodded toward the bell tower, he made a statement filled with ominous overtones: "If anything ever happens to me so as I can't come home, maybe this old bell will ring to let you know I love you true and couldn't help it."

Overwrought with emotion, Leona sobbed, "Johnny, you must come back, 'cause I can't live without you. I'm powerfully much in love with you!"

After a tender embrace, the time for parting was at hand. Johnny climbed atop Ned, his mule, waved farewell, and rode off to Raleigh, where would-be soldiers were gathering from every part of the state. Over the next four years, North Carolina would provide more soldiers and suffer more casualties than any other Southern state in the maelstrom that was to be the American Civil War.

During the first two years, the war was for the most part fought in places far away from Moore County. Like most of the soldiers North Carolina provided for the Confederacy, Johnny was sent to the battlegrounds of Virginia and points north. As the war grew in intensity and scope, so did the human losses. Almost daily, lists of killed and missing local boys were posted in Aberdeen. Leona was always there to anxiously scan the list to make sure that Johnny's name did not appear. She rarely heard from him by mail. It was not that he no longer cared. Rather, Johnny was not an accomplished writer. On the rare occasion when local soldiers came home on wounded furlough, they would deliver to Leona worn notes written by Johnny and stained with the sweat and grime of wartime campsites. On the home front, Leona and the other women of the community whiled away the lonely hours by busying themselves with the tasks necessary to maintain a successful war effort—farming, weaving, and child rearing.

As twilight descended on a hot summer afternoon in 1863 in the Sandhills region of North Carolina, Leona was taking the butter she had just churned to the springhouse when she heard the sorrowful sound. The bell at Old Bethesda was sounding a slow but loud knell. Leona forgot what she was about and dashed off toward the church. With each step she took, the ringing grew louder, clearer. She found it strange because it wasn't Sunday.

By the time Leona reached the church graveyard, she could

see that two men were standing in a state of bewilderment outside the church. Frantically, she ran up to them to find out what was going on. All they could tell her was that the building was locked tight. Perhaps a child had snuck inside and was pulling the rope to the bell.

There seemed to be no end to the ringing. One of the men finally pulled himself up the side of the building, unlocked a window, and made his way inside. When he emerged from the church, his face was as pale as a shirt. In a quivering voice, he stammered, "There's nobody in there. That bell is ringing by itself with the rope going up and down with each pull."

His words penetrated Leona's heart like a dagger. There was no question about it now—the tolling bell was a message from her dear Johnny that he would not be able to make it back home. He had kept the promise made on that fateful spring afternoon.

Darkness was now enveloping the church grounds. The torches carried by the multitude who had gathered at the church cast an eerie light. Finally, one of the members climbed the tower and stopped the phantom ringing.

Leona was not among the assembled crowd. Crushed by the revelation of the clanging bell, she had rushed home, where her aunt had consoled the weeping, brokenhearted teenager. Overcome with sorrow, Leona had cried out, "He's dead! He ain't coming back to me!"

For the next few days, the grief-stricken girl refused to leave her bed and did not eat or drink. Then a new casualty list was posted, and on it appeared the name of Johnny Blue. He had been killed in action in early July on the rocky Pennsylvania landscape at a place called Gettysburg.

Leona received the grim news quietly. To her, it was not news at all. The next day, she died in her sleep. Family and friends buried her in the cemetery at Old Bethesda and planted a yellow rosebush atop her grave. As for Johnny Blue, he was interred with his fallen Confederate comrades on that faraway battleground.

Since that sad summer day in 1863 in Aberdeen, the bell at Old Bethesda has rung on many occasions, but only when it was pulled by human hands. Some say that its supernatural tolling during the Civil War was a death knell. But if you're a romantic at heart, you will understand that the ghostly ringing was a grand celebration of a special, meant-to-be kind of love that could never die.

A Mystery within a Mystery

The most beautiful experience we can have is the mysterious. It is a fundamental emotion which stands at the cradle of art and science. Whoever does not know it can no longer wonder, no longer marvel, is as good as dead, and his eyes are dimmed.

Albert Einstein

Over the long history of North Carolina, some of the state's greatest mysteries have been solved. Nevertheless, there are others that linger without solution. These mysteries haunt historians, who have watched them become more shrouded in uncertainty and complexity as the years have passed. Some of them have been the genesis for mysteries within themselves. Such is the case with the disappearance of Theodosia Burr Alston in 1812.

Theodosia was the wife of John Alston, the governor of South Carolina, and the daughter of Aaron Burr, the third vice president of the United States. No one disputes that she was in

Georgetown, South Carolina, in late December 1812. Most historians believe she boarded *The Patriot* there near the end of that month for a trip to New York to visit her father, who had recently returned to America after a period of exile in Europe. Her subsequent disappearance has been attributed to the loss of the ship at sea or to attack and murder by pirates. There is, however, one theory that suggests Theodosia never boarded *The Patriot*. Instead, the theory goes, she chose to travel to New York by coach. At that time, the only north-south interstate stage route through North Carolina took passengers from Raleigh to Tarboro and then to points north. And therein lies our mystery within a mystery.

On a cold, blustery day in early January 1813, a luxurious carriage traveling the stage route north from Raleigh pulled up to the cabin of Mrs. Emmy Brantley in Samaria, a small community in northern Nash County. Mrs. Brantley's hound dogs, awakened from their sleep near the roaring fire, began to bark. The matron of the house cracked the door and peered outside to determine what was going on. Although many fine coaches and carriages passed her house, it was unusual for one to stop. Most travelers sojourned at the State Coach Inn, a few miles east.

Mrs. Brantley watched as a uniformed black driver jumped down from the most elaborate carriage she had ever laid eyes on. With his gloved hands, the coachman helped a frail woman of striking beauty from the coach. As the lady approached the cabin, Mrs. Brantley quickly discerned that she was a woman of nobility and refinement. She also noticed that the stranger was tightly clutching a bundle to her bosom.

That mysterious bundle turned out to be a baby. Without introducing herself, the well-bred lady looked at Mrs. Brantley with weak eyes and a pale face and said in a voice that combined courage and desperation, "I'm ill. When I'm well again, I'll return for it. Please give it a good home."

The kindly lady had little time to respond, as the baby was literally shoved into her arms. Looking alternately into the face of the infant boy and that of the visitor, the perplexed Mrs. Brantley asked, "What's its name?"

Unwilling to answer that query or any other, the child's mother took her leave by saying, "His name isn't important. Just love it." With those words, she was gone. Neither Mrs. Brantley nor the child ever saw or heard from her again.

Mrs. Brantley and her husband reared the child as their own. They named him Lovett. He grew into a fine young man who married his foster sister. When Lovett Brantley passed away at the age of fifty-five just after the Civil War, he died without knowing the identity of his natural parents. Or did he?

There are some who believe that the aristocratic lady who left Lovett at the Brantley household in Samaria that bitter January day was none other than Theodosia Burr Alston. Long before the child was born, John Alston's letters to Theodosia reflected his suspicious and inconsiderate attitude toward his wife. As the theory goes, Governor Alston's callous, demeaning treatment of Theodosia led her to engage in an illicit love affair that produced the child who grew up as Lovett Brantley.

Before you dismiss the idea as pure fiction, there is one other intriguing piece of the puzzle to consider. When Lovett was a young man, another stranger showed up in Samaria. According to people who saw him, he appeared to be a person of affluence and good breeding. Over the course of the next few days, the stranger met with Lovett in private, and the two engaged in lengthy conversations. Finally, just before the genteel man made his departure, he purchased a sizable tract of land for Lovett. Friends and neighbors were extremely curious, but Lovett never disclosed whether he knew the identity of his benefactor. Some have concluded that the man was his father.

You can find Lovett's grave in the Brantley family plot in the small cemetery approximately one mile north of Samaria. Close to his final resting place, you will see the grave of his loving foster mother. His natural mother disappeared into history. Was she Theodosia? Maybe Lovett took the answer to that mystery within a mystery to his grave here in Nash County.

The Haunting of Seven Hearths

Peeping in the windows, tapping on the doors,
Creeping, crawling, chilling things,
Scurrying over floors.

Unknown

Steeped in history and tradition, ancient Hillsborough is one of the oldest towns in the state. Incorporated in 1759, it was a politically prominent place before North Carolina became a state, and it subsequently played a major role in the movement toward statehood. During the Revolutionary War era, Hillsborough played host to the Third Provincial Congress (1775), the North Carolina General Assembly (1778, 1780, 1783, and 1784), and the Federal Constitutional Convention of 1788. A handsome collection of eighteenth-century homes can be found on the old streets laid out when George Washington was less than thirty years old.

Seven Hearths, located in the heart of town at 157 East King Street, is one of the oldest and finest of the early homes. Although the exact date of its construction is unknown, it was occupied as early as 1753 by William Reed, a court official. The well-maintained, five-level frame structure endures as an outstanding example of early Piedmont architecture. Among its most outstanding features are its massive chimneys, its seven fireplaces, and its two ghosts.

Ironically, the ghosts of Seven Hearths almost lost their haunt when the house was about two hundred years old. By the late 1950s, the dwelling had fallen into a bad state of repair after years of use as a rental property. Then along came Dr. and Mrs. Robert Murphy, who purchased it, moved in, and spent thirteen years restoring it to its former grandeur. During their ownership, both of the ghosts began to make regular appearances.

Of the two spectres, the more unusual is the cat-ghost. It was first encountered by Thelma, the family maid, one night while she was baby-sitting the Murphy children. When she opened the door to let the pet dogs out, they refused to cooperate, even though the weather was pleasant. Instead, they backed into the house as if in fear of something. Then Thelma saw the reason for their strange behavior. It was a cat, sitting on the porch, but it did not resemble any cat she had ever seen before. Thelma was unnerved because it looked just like Dr. Hayes, her former physician, who had been dead for years! Following this encounter, Thelma was forever uneasy when she was left alone in the house. She was especially afraid to go down to the basement, where she claimed to hear odd noises. Thelma had a stock response to those noises: "Dr. Hayes?"

When she related the bizarre occurrence to Mrs. Murphy, the lady of the house dismissed it as a flight of fancy. However, her disbelief was soon to change. One night as Dr. and Mrs. Murphy and their daughter, Karen, were sitting on the living-room sofa watching television, Karen gently nudged her mother to look at the big, red cat that had suddenly appeared at the glass door leading to the kitchen. What struck Mrs. Murphy about the cat was its big eyes filled with sadness. Feeling sorry for it, she got up to take a closer look. But after a thorough search, there was no cat to be found.

Bewildered by the incident, Mrs. Murphy received some answers on a subsequent night when John Bell, a local television repairman, stopped by the house. As they talked, their conversation turned to Dr. Hayes, the physician Thelma had supposedly seen in the form of a cat. As a youngster, Bell had also been treated by Dr. Hayes, who had once lived in and maintained his office in Seven Hearths. When he was ten years old, John Bell had been taken to Seven Hearths for treatment of a stomach ache. In the course of the examination, Dr. Hayes told young John something very curious: that the boy would someday turn into a horse. The doctor went on to describe his belief in reincarnation. According to Dr. Hayes, when someone dies, that person turns into an animal. If the individual was evil as a human being, he returns as a low form of animal, such as a snake. Conversely, a good, upright person can expect to return in a much higher form—a horse or the like.

Mrs. Murphy pondered this strange information. And then something happened that convinced her that Dr. Hayes had returned to his former home as a cat. One cold winter night when snow was falling in Hillsborough, the Murphy family heard pitiful meowing at the back door. When Mrs. Murphy went to the door, she was taken aback to see the big, red cat again. Because of the forlorn expression on its face and the snow on its fur, she felt sorry for the animal. She got some milk and meat from the nearby refrigerator, but by the time she got back to the door, the cat was gone. And there was no trace of it—not even tracks in the deep snow.

Miss Susan Hayes, the sister of the late physician, had occasion to visit Seven Hearths after the Murphys restored it. She scoffed at the idea that Dr. Hayes had returned to his former home as a cat-ghost. Nonetheless, Karen Murphy was certain of it. She noted that on every occasion she had seen the animal, it resembled a cat, save for one major feature. Its sad face, filled with expression, was that of a human.

Despite her reluctance to acknowledge her brother's reincarnation as a cat, Miss Hayes related to the Murphys her knowledge of another ghost at Seven Hearths. Jane Hayes was a sixteen-year-old girl who had died of consumption in her room in the attic in 1850. Miss Hayes noted that the girl, one of her ancestors, was small in stature and had long, blond hair. Mrs. Murphy and Karen were shocked at the revelation, for the description of Jane Hayes matched that of the ghostly figure Karen had encountered in various rooms at Seven Hearths. Karen had first observed the apparition when she was eleven. She was reading in the sitting room when she suddenly experienced the feeling that someone else was present. Looking up from her book, she fully expected to see her mother or sister. She was astonished, however, to witness the white, filmy-looking apparition of a little girl wearing a dressing gown. The ghost had curly, waist-length hair. It did not walk but rather floated above the floor and through the walls. On another occasion, the ghost manifested itself to Karen in an upstairs den. Pale and smoky in appearance, the apparition made its way past the scared girl and vanished into thin air.

Eventually, the Murphys sold Seven Hearths and moved away. But it appears that several members of the Hayes family have never wanted to leave. And so here they stay, whether in the form of a phantom cat with a human face or the ghost of a pretty teenager who died prematurely.

When Fear Was Real

Fear always remains. A man may destroy everything within himself, love and hate and belief, and even doubt; but as long as he clings to life, he cannot destroy fear.

Joseph Conrad

Throughout American history, no figure of the supernatural world has elicited more fear among children than the witch. Countless tiny Americans have been terrified by the mere description of the grotesque, repulsive hag and her evil powers. To little ones, the witch has always been the most believable creature of the netherworld because she is manifested in human form, unlike demons, ghosts, and monsters.

During the Reconstruction period in North Carolina, Tar Heel children gathered around fireplaces on chilly evenings to hear folk tales about witches from the distant past, when the practice of witchcraft was more widespread. When the morning sun ushered forth a new day, many of these youngsters ventured from their homes to look upon strange, eccentric, and poorly dressed local women. Their furtive imaginations, fueled by the fireside stories, ran wild. Those unsightly females, often attired in rags, must be witches!

Such was the state of affairs in the community of Concord in rural northeastern Person County in the years following the Civil War. Old witch tales abounded in the homes of farmers and planters making the difficult transition to the new postwar economy. The poverty here along the North Carolina-Virginia border may have played a part in leading local children to often mistake impoverished old women for witches. But in at least two instances, the intuition of the little ones might have been right.

Henry was a young son of the Wagstaff family, which had lost a considerable portion of its wealth during the war. Nonetheless, Henry's mother realized that there were many needy people in the community, and she was willing to share with them. One such underprivileged person was Betsy Boyd, better known to Henry as "Miss Betsy." She and her unmarried daughter, Jenny, had shown up one day from parts unknown. They took up residence in a crude cabin located on land belonging to Henry's uncle. There, they lived a reclusive life, eking out a meager existence from a small vegetable garden and from Jenny's work as a seamstress.

Henry considered Miss Betsy strange in both appearance and behavior. Whenever he saw her, she was most often poking about on a hobble-stick. In every way, she had the look of a witch, from her stooped frame in its dark clothes to her head in its slatted poke-bonnet.

Two or three days a week, Jenny did some sewing at Henry's house. She always left with a nice supply of household goods given to her by Mrs. Wagstaff. On other occasions, a carriage dispatched from the Wagstaff place delivered items to Miss Betsy.

Then came the day when Mrs. Wagstaff summoned Henry

and his brother to deliver a pail of butter to Miss Betsy. Her cabin was approximately a mile away. Off they went, Henry's brother—the older of the two—carrying the bucket.

When they were in sight of their destination, little Henry requested that they stop for a brief rest on the overgrown path. As they caught their breath, the boys noticed an old woman standing on a hill some fifty yards away. She held a walking stick in one hand while using the other to pick plums. Henry's brother called to her, recognizing her to be Miss Betsy. But as soon as he did, she was gone. Bewildered by the sudden disappearance, the boys turned toward the cabin, only to see Miss Betsy standing in its open doorway.

The terrified Henry pleaded, "Let's go back."

In an attempt to mask his own fear, the older boy responded, "But Miss Betsy needs the butter."

Henry grabbed the pail, put it on a nearby stump, and goaded his brother into flight with these words: "You watch while I travel."

With that, the boys sped off in the direction of their farm. Emboldened by the welcome sight of the Wagstaff residence, Henry's brother reminded him that a witch could not harm them in broad daylight. Nevertheless, they maintained a rapid pace until they reached the front gate.

Although their mother teased the boys that they had been listening to too many tales, they were convinced from that day forward that Miss Betsy was a witch. They were never willing to visit her cabin again. As adults, they remained firm in the belief that they had witnessed the supernatural. As Henry put it, "Both of us were ever beyond question in the faith that Miss Betsy on that day was either in two places at once or else bridged the distance of one hundred yards in the bat of an eye." Indeed, Henry McGilbert Wagstaff was very much aware of the difference between fact and superstition. He served with great distinction as professor of history at the University of North Carolina at Chapel Hill from 1907 until his death in 1945. That Old Betsy was a Person County witch was fact to Henry. His long-held belief was seconded by Edmund, an old servant on the Wagstaff estate. Upon being informed of the bizarre incident soon after it happened, Edmund looked at Henry and remarked, "Miss Betsy surely is a witch. I wonder, can she conjure us by jes' looking?"

Little Henry never had the nerve to ascertain the answer to that question, but some other Person County children found out in a horrifying way when they ran afoul of a different witch. This group of children made the mistake of poking fun at the evil, squinting eyes and the humped back of a frail black woman as she labored with a hoe in the fields. Their incessant ridicule continued day after day until one afternoon when Ada, as the woman was called, spotted them around the corner of a tobacco packing house. Unable to restrain her anger, she grabbed several of the youngsters and violently shook them, then clawed another. Before they could scamper away, Ada—her "terrible eyes flashing fire," as one witness put it—screamed that they would all die sudden and horrible deaths.

When the children informed their parents, Ada was summarily fired from her work as a field hand. As she walked away, some people heard her remark that all involved would be punished. Nobody paid much attention to what they considered the mumbling of a bitter, frustrated old woman.

As time passed, no one really thought about Ada, save the children who had incurred her wrath. Then, one day, a little girl who had played a part in teasing the woman was stricken with a mysterious illness and died without warning. Soon afterward, another of Ada's youthful tormenters died in much the same manner.

Fear spread throughout the community. Parents took measures to ensure the safety of their children. A group of fathers paid a visit to Ada at her cabin in the forest. There, they encountered the evil, horrifying eyes that their children had experienced. When questioned about the sudden rash of deaths, the woman remarked that the children were responsible for their own misfortune. While she was speaking, a huge owl found a perch on her shoulder. At that moment, not a person at the cabin doubted that Ada was a witch. Seizing rails from a nearby fence, the outraged men sought to kill her, but Ada suddenly rose and flapped away like a giant bird. The astonished vigilantes saw her light in the top of a nearby pine tree. As night descended on Person County, maniacal laughter sounded from the tree.

For many days thereafter, the diabolical laughter echoed throughout the community. At length, some families moved away.

From Person County, we can learn a valuable lesson in the supernatural: While witches are the most spooky of all evil creatures to children, it is children who are best able to identify them. Perhaps they know better than adults that there are real witches who live outside the pages of fairy tales.

The Hunter at the Zoo

I do not fear the explosive power of the atom bomb. What I fear is the explosive power of evil in the human heart.

Albert Einstein

Purgatory Mountain, a nine-hundred-foot peak in central Randolph County, is best known as the location of the North Carolina Zoological Park. Little did state officials realize when they chose this rugged terrain as the site of one of the finest natural-habitat zoos in the world that it was haunted by the ghost of an evil hunter. Today, the myriad animals that call the zoo home may be frightened on occasion by the malevolent ghost that roams there. But they are safe from his gun and knife, for the hunter at the zoo tracks only humans.

This story dates from the beginning of the Civil War, when much of this portion of Randolph County was an enclave of Quakers. These peace-loving citizens disdained military service because of their deep religious beliefs and their repugnance of war and killing. As a result, few volunteered to fight for either army in the great maelstrom that was to engulf the divided nation.

To the chagrin of many local residents, a recruiter for the Confederate army was dispatched to the area in the early stages of the war. After the recruiter established his office, much of the Quakers' bitterness subsided, because the man was very likable and conducted his business and personal affairs in an honest, reputable, and agreeable manner. His three-year stint of duty was without incident, although he was never very successful in bringing local men into the fold of the Southern army.

Near the close of the war, when the Confederate cause was in need of every able-bodied male to bolster its ebbing fortunes, a new recruiter was assigned to the Purgatory Mountain area. Unlike his predecessor, the newcomer was a vile, contemptible person who showed no respect or tolerance toward the people in the area. Quakers who refused his demands to don the gray uniform of the Confederacy were subjected to ridicule and humiliation. The recruiter roamed the countryside armed with gun and knife. In the presence of women and girls, he behaved crudely and showed great disrespect.

But it was when he and his nefarious assistants initiated a reign of terror in central and southern Randolph County that the recruiter gained his infamous nickname, "the Hunter." The name came about after he and his associates gathered by armed force a group of twenty-two local boys, all under the age of thirteen, and marched them to a Confederate compound in Wilmington. Neighbors were outraged to see the boys tied together as they set out on the long forced march in the middle of December.

During the tiring journey, the captives discussed the possibility of escape. Not long after their arrival in eastern North Carolina, they took advantage of a lack of guards to perfect their break. By the time the emaciated boys returned to Randolph County, more than two months had passed since their roundup by the Hunter. Throughout their harrowing experience, they had endured bitterly cold temperatures, snowstorms without shelter, swollen rivers and creeks without boats, and days and nights with little or no food.

The escapees reckoned that it would not be wise to immediately return to their homes. They reasoned that the Hunter would come back for his elusive prey. And sure enough, the recruiter had learned of the escape and was already in the process of searching their homes and violating their families. Accordingly, the boys separated and hid in various spots in the wilderness of Purgatory Mountain. Under cover of night, they made their way back to their homes to communicate with their loved ones and to obtain rations.

Under the starry skies one winter midnight, all the boys assembled along Panther Creek at the base of the mountain to plot the extermination of the Hunter. Three of their number—the best marksmen—were chosen to study the daily routine of their hated adversary. Then they were to seek him out and destroy him.

In a matter of days, all was ready. At first light one frosty morning, the three sharpshooters positioned themselves behind the Hunter's house at the foot of the mountain. When he emerged from his cabin, two well-directed shots broke the early-morning stillness. He fell dead in his tracks. Hastily, the ambushers made their way to the lifeless body to ensure that they had completed their mission. To prove that they had taken their prize, the boys stripped the brass buttons from the Hunter's Confederate uniform.

Not long after the attack at Purgatory Mountain, the Civil War ended. For as long as they lived, none of the boys disclosed their deadly secret. Folks in the neighborhood never seemed to question the identity of the persons who rid Purgatory Mountain of its menace.

But were the youngsters actually successful in their quest? For years, there have been numerous reports that the spirit of the Hunter haunts Purgatory Mountain. His ghost is said to wander the rocky outcrops in a relentless effort to exact revenge for his murder. Most often, the apparition is observed around sunrise, just about the time his body was riddled by bullets.

As you meander the North Carolina Zoological Park admiring the animals from distant parts of the earth, bear this in mind: the Hunter yet prowls the landscape, intending to continue the evil he began so long ago at a place ominously called Purgatory Mountain.

The Warlock
by the River

Evil, therefore, is a fact not to be explained away, but to be accepted, and accepted not to be endured, but to be conquered.

John Hayes Holmes

There is a widespread belief, even among some pragmatists and skeptics, that there is a mysterious force of evil at work in the world. Evil—the aggregate of all things wrong, wicked, bad, and immoral—often manifests itself in everyday life without the identity of the perpetrator being known. On the other hand, when an evildoer is identified or apprehended, that person is brought to justice. It is thanks to civil and criminal laws, religious doctrines, and social mores that an individual cannot practice evil on a regular basis in civilized society.

Throughout history, there have been wicked persons possessed of strange, supernatural powers who have practiced their special brand of evil virtually unchecked. They have used their sorcery for self-aggrandizement and to inflict pain and suffering on their enemies. No satisfactory explanation has surfaced for the source of their unearthly powers. Some of these evil creatures have been accused of being in league with the devil himself.

The female practitioner of sorcery has long been known as a witch. Her male counterpart is called a warlock. One of the most famous of all warlocks in the annals of North Carolina lived in Richmond County many years ago. His name was Harvey, and he resided in a hovel along the bank of the Pee Dee River a few miles west of Rockingham, the county seat. Harvey was an old man when he settled here. Over time, he became acquainted with the people who lived on the neighboring farms. Many initially looked upon the hobbling old man with pity. As a consequence, they acceded to his requests for items such as flour and sugar. But then his demands grew.

One morning, Harvey called on his neighbor, Miss Sally, while she was milking her prized cow. Out of the blue, the old man asked her to give the animal to him. Without hesitation, Sally refused, which caused Harvey to close his eyes in disgust. As he turned to totter back down the path to his shanty, he groused, "You'd much better give her to me, for she'll never do you a spoonful of good."

Sally chuckled at the babbling of what she considered a senile old fool. The following morning, however, she was greatly dismayed to discover that her cow gave blood rather than milk. Her concern mounted as, day after day, the animal refused to eat, gave no milk, and lost weight. Finally, at her wit's end, Sally delivered the cow to Harvey for fear that he might be a warlock.

Concerned about the well-being of the animal, she walked over to Harvey's place the morning after she bestowed her gift. There, much to her astonishment, was the old man milking the cow while it voraciously devoured some oats. In a nearby pail, Sally saw a large quantity of rich, foaming milk. Outraged by Harvey's behavior, she belittled him and indicated her intention to reclaim her cow. But when Harvey warned her that the animal would most likely die before she got it home, Sally decided not to further test his evil powers. Instead, she admonished Harvey never to come about her property again.

For several weeks, the wizard obeyed the injunction. Then, one morning, he approached Miss Sally, who was in the process of feeding her very rotund pig. When she saw Harvey standing there with covetous eyes, Sally ordered him to leave. Harvey gave her an unearthly stare and proclaimed, "I'll go, but you'd better give me that nice little hog!"

Her courage and anger mounting, Sally screamed, "You durned old witch, I'll give you a load of shot if you don't leave here right now. You cheated me out of a cow, and you'll get nothing else out of me."

Undaunted, Harvey gave a wicked laugh and announced, "If you don't give me that hog, it'll never do you any good." With that, he departed.

Sally walked over to pet her pig, uttering words to the effect that the "old devil" could do it no harm. But as soon as Harvey entered the forest that separated his home from Sally's farm, the hog keeled over dead!

Terrified by thoughts of what the evil man might do next, Sally tearfully buried the animal, then sought the advice of her neighbors. One man directed her to draw a figure of the warlock, then shoot it in the part of the body where she wanted the old man to experience pain. When she was satisfied that he had suffered sufficiently, she should take the picture down, after which Harvey would regain his health. Anxious to try the suggestion, Sally hurried home, drew a full-body likeness of Harvey, affixed it to an outbuilding, and opened fire.

A day later, she paid a visit to the warlock's hut, where, to her delight, she found him confined to bed with a terrible pain in his shoulder—the exact spot where Sally had shot the picture.

Day after day, Sally shot the figure and Harvey suffered great discomfort in the same part of the body. Convinced that the warlock was being justly punished, she felt no guilt in what she did.

On one occasion, however, Sally discovered on her daily visit that Harvey was in very serious condition. Reckoning that she had exacted a sufficient measure of revenge, she decided to remove the drawing. But as she began to walk toward the outbuilding where it hung, the sky darkened and fierce winds began to blow. Fearing the powerful storm, Sally ran to the safety of her house with the intention of removing the picture the following morning.

Inside her dwelling, she shook in fear as terrible lightning streaked across the sky and thunder resonated along the Pee Dee. Suddenly, a jagged bolt struck the outbuilding to which was attached the likeness of Harvey. The resulting fire reduced the structure to ashes within minutes. "Perhaps," she thought to herself, "Harvey will now recover."

But when Sally arrived at the old man's cabin early the next morning, she was shocked to see a large gathering of her neighbors. Informed that Harvey was dying, she rushed inside just as the warlock's weakened voice offered his last wish: "I know I've been an evil man, but I have one last request to make. I will die this morning, and I want you to bury me between my dog and my mule under the walnut tree in the field. They are the only things that ever loved me. Bury me right after dinner, and when the lightning strikes the tree, you'll know I'm in hell." Harvey took one last choking breath and then expired.

In the early afternoon, he was buried at the place he had requested. His neighbors then quickly departed in hopes of reaching their homes before an impending storm struck. At length, rain fell in torrents, wind raised whitecaps on the Pee Dee, the sky groaned with thunder, and a deadly streak of lightning hit the walnut tree at Harvey's grave.

Harvey the warlock was no more. Local folks insist that the storm sent the wicked man straight to a meeting with the devil. The stump of that walnut tree stood on the bank of the river for many years as a grim reminder of the supernatural evil that once tormented the people of the Pee Dee.

Ghostly Legacy of the Swamp Fox

Remember thee!
Ay, thou poor ghost, while memory holds a seat
In this distracted globe.

William Shakespeare

Winding south from its headwaters at the Moore County-Richmond County line to its junction with the Pee Dee River just south of the South Carolina line, the majestic Lumber River is one of the most unspoiled waterways in all of North Carolina. Much of the shoreline of this 125-mile, free-flowing, blackwater river is as undeveloped as it was when America was fighting for its independence. Snaking along the Robeson County line, the southern quarter of the river offers spectacular vistas of cypress gum swamps and bottom-land hardwoods within the confines of Lumber River State Park.

General Francis Marion, one of the most legendary heroes of the American Revolution, is most often associated with the lowlands of South Carolina. But on occasion, the Swamp Fox and his guerrilla warriors set up camp in the swamps along the Lumber River in Robeson County. The ghosts of a man and woman who died on the gallows at one of Marion's camps here are said to linger near the river.

At the outbreak of the Revolutionary War, the Highland Scots who had poured into southeastern North Carolina faced a dilemma: should they honor the Oath of Culloden and maintain their allegiance to the British Crown, or should they fight for the freedom of North Carolina and the other colonies? The majority of these Highlanders chose to remain loyal to Great Britain. This chilling story of two lovers, Walter Jenkins and Jean McDougald, recounts the ghostly consequences when such loyalties were tested.

One day, deep within a South Carolina swamp near the North Carolina line, Joan and Walter shared a romantic embrace. Walter whispered to her, "I've taken a great chance in meeting you. If Marion's men knew, it would mean my life."

Joan shuddered to think of the risks Walter was taking because of his love for her. On several occasions, the handsome young man, considered one of the best noncommissioned officers in the Swamp Fox's command, had given Joan's father, an avowed Tory, important information about planned attacks by General Marion.

As he prepared to depart, Walter kissed her and said, "I must go. They mustn't suspect me at camp."

Determined to obtain the intelligence needed by her father, Joan called out in desperation as Walter mounted his horse, "Wait! Walter, if Marion plans a raid, please let me know. We are prepared for whatever may happen. Last night, father said that upon the enemy's next move, we will go to North Carolina."

Walter acknowledged her request and rode off into the darkness.

The next night, Joan was awakened by an owl-like hoot, Walter's prearranged signal. She hurriedly dressed and hastened to his side.

Joan had never before seen such a look on his face. His eyes expressed concern bordering on fear, and his voice was filled with desperation. "Joan, you must hurry!" he said. "Our forces are massed for an attack on the settlement. Marion plans to be here by noon tomorrow!"

Joan could muster only a short sentence before Walter climbed back upon his horse: "I must tell father."

Walter bent down from his saddle to hug her. "May God protect you," he declared.

As the sergeant galloped away, Joan sounded the alarm to Captain Sam McDougald—her father—and the other Tories at the temporary settlement. Before daybreak, they were on the move to North Carolina. Once across the line, the Highlanders settled in a swamp located between the Lumber and Waccamaw Rivers at a place still known as Tory Island. There, they quickly put up a makeshift fort.

Upon learning that General Marion's army had likewise entered North Carolina, Captain McDougald was anxious to receive details of the enemy's whereabouts. Calling his daughter to his side, he implored, "Take a fast horse, Joan. Slip into the camp of the Whigs and persuade the sergeant to warn of his assault."

"But Father, I fear for his safety," Joan pleaded. "At our last meeting, he told me Marion suspected someone of giving information. And I know it must hurt him to betray his superiors."

Confident that he would prevail, Captain McDougald challenged his daughter's loyalty: "Very well, then, the safety of your rebel lover comes before your loyalty to the clan. God forbid that I should have raised such a daughter."

Unable to turn her back on her father and her people, Joan

mounted a fleet horse. After riding for miles, she located Marion's camp, where most of the soldiers were asleep. Maintaining a safe distance, the young woman sounded the owl-like signal to Walter. In an instant, he held her in his arms. After a passionate kiss, Sergeant Jenkins asked why she had come to a place of such danger.

"Walter, I want you to save my people," she beseeched. "I have come to you for protection and help. Won't you ride ahead and inform us the hour of Marion's attack?"

Walter agreed, though he feared it might cost him his life.

Tears of gratitude poured from Joan's eyes as she pulled Walter close. "Thank God," she sobbed. "We are too few to fight but too many to die."

Before the infatuated pair took leave of each other, Walter announced his plan: "Have your father put guards on the trail leading to the island. If an order to attack is given, I will ride and tell them for your sake. You must leave now."

When the Tory guards went to their posts along the trail the following night, Joan stayed in a tent along the route in order to see Walter if he brought news of the attack. Midnight came and went, but there was no sleep for Joan. Finally, in the early hours of the morning, one of the guards came to the tent and informed her that a horseman was in the nearby clearing.

The full moon offered just enough light for her to recognize Walter. She rushed to him as he was dismounting. In a frantic voice, he said, "Joan, Marion plans."

Those three words were all he spoke before a round of gunfire provided a violent interruption. Marion's soldiers poured out of the darkness from all sides. "Traitor!" their leader screamed.

Sergeant Jenkins was taken into custody. As he was being led away by the Patriots, Joan found herself overcome with emotion and guilt. Tearfully, she cried out, "Oh, Walter, what have I done?"

General Marion soon launched a savage attack on Tory Island, during which his warriors razed the fort and houses there. In the aftermath of the assault, Captain McDougald and his fellow Scots returned and established a temporary camp at the site.

Poor Joan, suffering from remorse, could not be left alone for fear that she might harm herself. Her mental state approached madness. She constantly saw Walter's face, and the sounds of owls gave her false hope that he was calling her. At length, Joan could tolerate her misery no longer. Under the cloak of darkness, she stole away from Tory Island and rode through the wilderness to Marion's camp in the swamps along the Lumber River. Dismounting from her horse, she approached quietly until she saw that the camp had been abandoned.

But what the Swamp Fox had left behind was horrifying. The bright moon, shining down like a spotlight, revealed a recently constructed scaffold. Swinging from a rope was a lifeless body— that of Sergeant Walter Jenkins.

Joan screamed at the garish sight and stepped onto the platform. Gathering up a piece of rope, she fashioned a noose and joined her lover in death on the gallows.

Even now, when the moon beams down on the Lumber River in Robeson County, it is said that two ghost-like figures can be observed in the swamp at the site of the Swamp Fox's former camp. One of the apparitions is thought to be the ever-faithful Walter, pledging his love, and the other is Joan, pleading for forgiveness.

The Incident at Settle's Bridge

Men say that in this midnight hour,
The disembodied have power.

William Matherwell

There's something special about covered bridges. They are associated with romantic, idyllic scenes that harken back to simpler times. Sadly, these antiquated structures are vanishing from the American landscape. For example, as late as 1936, North Carolina boasted fifty-six covered bridges. Today, it has but three.

Settle's Bridge, one of the most picturesque covered bridges in North Carolina, fell victim to progress in 1952. Constructed in 1871 to span the Dan River approximately three miles northwest of Wentworth, the seat of Rockingham County, the bridge was named for Thomas Settle, Jr., a local politician who was elected to the North Carolina Supreme Court. It was alternately known as the Dead Timbers Bridge for the nearby ford of the same name. Upon its completion, Settle's Bridge stood atop three massive stone pillars thirty-one feet above the river's low-water mark. Its roof was designed to protect the internal timbers from the elements and to extend the life of the structure. The covered portion of the span was three hundred feet long.

A public hanging in Rockingham County in early 1882 led to a mysterious incident at Settle's Bridge that would forever make the site a most haunted place. The events leading up to the haunting are well documented. On the night of December 17, 1880, Nash Carter, a middle-aged black shoemaker from Madison, was murdered by strangulation. During a snowstorm the night after his death, Carter's murderers removed his body to Stokes County, where it was not discovered until January 8, 1881. Were it not for a bit of the victim's hair found in a gate along the route to Stokes County, the crime might never have been solved. The authorities arrested Carter's wife, Tilda, and three of her male friends—Alfred Webster, Elridge Scales, and Joe Hayes—and charged them with murder.

When the case came to trial on December 1, 1881, Alfred Webster testified for the prosecution in order to avoid the noose. Based upon his testimony and other incriminating evidence, Tilda Carter, Scales, and Hayes were convicted of murder. They were sentenced to die by hanging on January 13, 1882, between the hours of ten in the morning and two in the afternoon.

On the appointed day, the three condemned prisoners were delivered to the gallows erected near the county poorhouse approximately one mile east of Wentworth. A crowd of several thousand people assembled to witness the grim spectacle. Before the black hoods were placed over their heads, all three of the murderers confessed. Then a noose was tightened around the neck of each, and they were put to death simultaneously in a bizarre triple hanging.

When the lifeless body of Tilda Carter was cut down from the gallows, it was claimed by a local physician, who planned to take it to his office, where he would use it for medical research. He placed the corpse on his horse and struck out for home. By the time the doctor reached Settle's Bridge, darkness had overtaken him. To make matters worse, a cold, soaking rain was falling. He decided to spend the night under the shelter of the bridge.

After the physician led his corpse-laden horse on to the span, no one knows for sure what happened. That the good doctor endured an evening of terror is beyond dispute. Those who knew him lamented that he was never the same afterward. But no one was ever able to persuade him to discuss his experiences that dark, cold January night.

Soon after the hanging, reports began to circulate that the ghost of Tilda Carter haunted the bridge. Thereafter, many locals refused to cross the river at night for fear of encountering the ghost of the executed woman.

On November 30, 1933, a forty-three-year-old state highway employee was killed in an accident on the bridge. His automobile mysteriously broke through the rail and plunged twenty-five feet. The hapless driver was crushed to death. Could it be that he witnessed the ghost of Tilda Carter just before his vehicle veered off the bridge?

In 1950, Settle's Bridge was declared unsafe by state officials. It was closed a year later upon the completion of a modern span six hundred feet upstream. Soon thereafter, the old covered bridge was dismantled and its stone pillars dynamited. Today, only a few scattered stones remain of the haunted bridge over the Dan.

There are some who say that Tilda's ghost disappeared once the covered bridge was no more. Others are not so sure. To see for yourself, you can drive over the replacement bridge on SR 2146 on a dark night and gaze downstream for Tilda. That is, if you dare.

The Murderer Who Refused to Die

Now comes the mystery.

Henry Ward Beecher

Old Dutch Second Creek, now identified on maps as South Second Creek, rises in southern Rowan County and courses into that portion of the Yadkin River known as High Rock Lake. Several years after the Civil War, the picturesque creek was the backdrop for one of the most bewildering stories in the annals of North Carolina.

Rufus Ludwig was a strong, able-bodied eighteen-year-old when North Carolina joined the Confederate States of America on May 20, 1861. At a time when most young men his age in Rowan County and throughout the state were stepping forward to fight for the South, Rufus shirked responsibility. His family background was not one of patriotism, but rather one of crime and violence. One of his cousins was an outlaw. Another had been hanged for murder. And his uncle had been hanged for killing his wife.

Folks who lived along the Yadkin shook their heads in disgust when Rufus mangled his hand with a self-inflicted gunshot in order to avoid military service at a time when North Carolina needed every soldier it could muster.

Despite his reputation as a ne'er-do-well, Rufus used his guile and charm to gain the love of Comilla Campbell, the daughter of one of the area's most prominent families. When Rufus and Comilla married, the bride's family disowned her, and the young couple moved in with Ludwig's parents. As far as anyone knew, the newlyweds lived a normal life for the first five months of their marriage. But then, on a Sunday in the spring of 1868, Comilla disappeared. For days, no trace of her was found. When asked about her whereabouts, Rufus said he had given her fifty cents on the morning of her disappearance and that she had gone to visit her parents.

As time passed and there was still no word from Comilla, suspicion grew that Rufus had killed her. When some local fishermen found her lifeless body in the muddy Yadkin several miles from the Ludwig home, local citizens' worst fears were realized. Comilla had died from a rifle shot to the back of the head. Rufus was promptly arrested and incarcerated for the murder, though he maintained his innocence. The authorities believed he had shot Comilla as she was fishing on the banks of Dutch Second Creek that Sunday morning.

One day, a wily Rowan County constable visited him in his jail cell and posed this question: "Rufus, why did you throw your wife's body in the river?"

Momentarily caught off guard, Rufus shot back, "I didn't. I threw it in the creek."

As soon as he said it, Rufus knew he had made a terrible mistake. He tried to shift some of the blame to his mother, Dicio Ludwig. According to Rufus's story, she had suggested that he and Comilla go fishing at the creek on the morning of the murder. As Rufus walked out of the house, his mother had handed him a loaded rifle and given him a stern admonition: "You'd better not bring her back with you." Rufus had obliged.

Rufus Ludwig was convicted of first-degree murder following a brief trial. He was sentenced to die by hanging.

On the appointed day, thousands of people from the Yadkin River Valley descended upon Salisbury, the seat of Rowan County, to witness the execution of a murderer from a family of rogues and killers. When Rufus was brought to the gallows, he made a desperate and futile attempt to escape. Soon, the trapdoor fell, the noose tightened, and the murderer dangled in front of the massive crowd. A physician hurried forward to examine the body. Rufus was officially declared to be dead.

Local officials escorted the body to the family cemetery near the Ludwig homestead, where a grave had been prepared. Without delay, the coffin was lowered and the opening covered with earth. One member of the escort detail, Dr. C. M. Poole, noted that he heard what seemed to be knocking sounds coming from the coffin as the grave was being closed. But no one paid any attention to him.

Exactly two weeks after the public hanging and burial of Rufus Ludwig, the law firm of Bailey and McCorkle received a curious letter. The attorneys who had been assigned to defend Rufus were shocked to read this:

Dear Sirs:

I am under many obligations for your efforts in my behalf, but I find there is more dependence to be put in slack ropes and shallow graves than in lawyers.

Thank you.

Rufus Ludwig

In the attorneys' judgment, the handwriting appeared to be that of the executed murderer. They turned the letter over to law enforcement. Concerned that the letter might be a cruel prank, the authorities paid a visit to the Ludwig farm. Strangely, the home was boarded up and abandoned. And when they opened the grave of the murderer, the coffin was empty. Rufus Ludwig was gone, and he was never seen again.

Booger Hill

We must not allow the clock and calendar to blind us to the fact that each moment of life is a miracle and mystery.

H. G. Wells

A paranormal phenomenon, a scientific anomaly, a gravitational mystery spot, an optical illusion—no matter what you call it, the mysterious force at work at the intersection of SR 1613 (Stewartsville Cemetery Road) and SR 1619 (Old Maxton Road) near the community of Johns in southeastern Scotland County sure is weird. At this haunted spot, a bizarre thing happens when you stop at the bottom of the hill on SR 1613 and put your car in neutral: an unknown force pushes your vehicle up the hill.

For decades, this spooky intersection has been known to locals as Booger Hill or Gravity Hill. Youngsters and adults alike flock to the site close to the South Carolina border to experience the strange effect for themselves. Many teenagers prefer to come late at night, due to the haunted aura that surrounds the place. Every Halloween night, vehicles stretch bumper to bumper for half a mile along SR 1613 to test the phenomenon.

One lady who resides near the intersection is familiar with the unearthly tales associated with the spot. "People call it Booger Hill," she admits. "I say, 'Don't call it that because I have to live here.' "

Stewartsville Cemetery Road runs downhill for almost a half-mile before it intersects Old Maxton Road. At the intersection, most motorists pull out beyond the stop sign to get a good view of any oncoming traffic. At that point, the force at work on Booger Hill takes over. If the driver puts his vehicle in neutral and takes his foot off the brake, his automobile will not roll forward into SR1613, as one would expect. Instead, it will roll backwards and up the hill, apparently in defiance of the laws of gravity.

In addition to Booger Hill in Scotland County, there are more than a dozen gravitational mystery spots in the United States. The other three in North Carolina have been commercialized as Mystery Hill at Blowing Rock, Mystery Shack at Maggie Valley, and Mystery House at Cherokee.

Scientists have studied these strange places, including Booger Hill. They believe there is a rational explanation. According to physicists, Booger Hill and other similar mysterious places involve a stretch of ground that is on a slight decline. Most often, the level horizon is obscured by objects such as trees and plants, which may be leaning slightly. This causes an optical illusion that makes a downhill slope appear to be an uphill slope.

In 1996, a physics professor at St. Andrews Presbyterian College in the nearby county seat of Laurinburg paid a visit to Booger Hill to study the mysterious intersection. After he made some measurements of the landscape, the professor concluded that the above theory postulated by scientists was applicable to this freaky place.

But local residents don't buy it. To them, seeing is believing. They are used to witnessing heavy trucks come to a complete stop, then roll in the opposite direction for seventy feet. Area folks are sure that a mysterious force, and not an optical illusion, is at work.

One possible explanation is the two horrible accidents that occurred here. In the waning days of the Civil War, a portion of General William T. Sherman's sixty-thousand-man army pushed across the North Carolina border in this area. A runaway horse and buggy killed two of the soldiers as they were crossing the intersection at Booger Hill. Their ghosts are said to still be present. At a much later date, a young woman pulled her automobile beyond the stop sign on SR 1613 to look in both directions on SR 1619. Her car stalled. When she got out to check under the hood, a fast-moving vehicle swung around the curve on SR 1619 and collided with her. She died as a result of the accident. Her ghost, too, has lingered at the scene.

In recent years, many an unwary motorist who has pulled too far into the intersection has been helped by these three ghosts, who gently but firmly push vehicles back up the hill and out of harm's way. Indeed, most people drive away from Booger Hill firm in the belief that it is aptly named.

A Perscription
for Terror

They are neither man nor woman—
They are neither brute nor human,
They are Ghouls!

Edgar Allen Poe

Morrow Mountain State Park, a majestic 4,135-acre recreational area located in eastern Stanly County in the mysterious Uwharrie Mountains, provides a perfect setting for a story about ghouls, ghosts, and buried treasure. Topping out at just over one thousand feet, the tallest peaks in the park are but a shadow of what they once were. Before time and erosion took their toll on these hills, they rivaled the Rockies and the Swiss Alps in height and grandeur. Some geologists have posited that the Uwharries are 500 million years old, making them possibly the oldest mountains in all of North America. At the state park, visitors are treated to a rugged wilderness area in the heart of the North Carolina Piedmont. Hiking trails afford panoramic vistas of lush, green forests, breathtaking gorges along the Pee Dee River, and the ravines and hills of the once-towering mountains.

Almost swallowed up by the vastness of this ancient place are the restored house, the clinic, and the outbuildings of Dr. Francis Joseph Kron, a European physician who lived here for nearly fifty years. Although Kron was liked and respected by the many people he cared for in Stanly and the surrounding counties, some said that he possessed supernatural powers as a result of his association with spirits, witches, demons, and the like. The doctor's sinister side, as this story will reveal, has allowed his hidden cache of gold to remain undisturbed since it was buried in the haunted Uwharries in 1878.

Born in Prussia in 1798, Kron was a teenager when his homeland fell under the control of France as a result of Napoleon's campaign in Germany in 1813. Kron followed the French back to Paris, where he obtained his medical education. On September 23, 1823, less than four months after Kron married a French lady, Mary Catherine Delamonthe, the newlyweds boarded a ship to America, which beckoned with the promise of a new life in an uncrowded land. Five months after their arrival, Dr. Kron was teaching French at the University of North Carolina.

In early 1827, the Krons moved to Montgomery County to be near Mary Catherine's uncle, who owned more than six thousand acres in the Uwharries. Over the next seven years, two daughters were born to the couple. Finally, in 1834, the Kron family decided to establish permanent roots in the area by purchasing a homestead in Stanly County. Kron's diary describes that happy event: "On the 2nd of November, 1834, I became proprietor of the place we now live—for the first time a landowner in America. . . . The plantation is on the west side of the Yadkin, a mile from Kirk's Ferry, the same distance south of the great falls of the Yadkin, on the market road from Salisbury to Fayetteville."

Kron's home, office, and ancillary structures were of log construction, as was typical for that time period. His dwelling stood atop a hill between two mountains—Mount Hathaway to the south and Fall Mountain to the north. Intensely interested in horticulture, Dr. Kron set about turning his homestead into a showplace of nature, replete with orchards, flowers, and a manicured lawn, a rarity at that time in rural North Carolina.

From his cozy outpost here, the doctor traveled countless miles by horse and buggy to render medical care to patients as far away as Salisbury. His crude clinic at his homestead was the closest thing to a hospital for many miles. He stocked his shelves with medicines and remedies, including some of his own concoctions, such as Dr. Kron's Pills. Although his fees—ten dollars for delivering a baby and fifty cents for extracting a tooth—were extremely low when compared with twenty-first-century medical costs, Dr. Kron is believed to have amassed a fortune from the sheer volume of his practice. Yet there was gossip that he often resorted to unorthodox forms of treatment, doling out unusual herbs and powders and chanting unintelligible gibberish while attending patients.

Kron was a private man who valued the solitude of his homestead. One of his diary entries reflects his abiding interest in passing his tranquil paradise in the Uwharries to his heirs: "By degrees as our means will allow, everything that is convenient will be put around us so that when death or fortune withdraws us from this our home, we shall at least leave a comfortable one to our successors."

Kron died in 1883. He was interred in a small family cemetery near his house. Perhaps the chilling events that had transpired on the plantation one autumn night in 1878 were in anticipation of his death and in accordance with his desire to take care of his heirs.

On that fateful night, Dan Compton, a lanky man employed by the physician to do odd jobs, was led into a dark room in the

Kron dwelling. There, Compton saw a huge keg in the center of the room. Kron directed him to roll the heavy keg out of the cabin and down to the middle of a field north of Mount Hathaway.

As he struggled to move the barrel, Compton clearly heard the clinking of coins inside. Midway between the house and the field, Kron granted permission for the thoroughly exhausted man to rest. During the brief respite, Compton saw through the cracks in the staves that the keg was loaded with gold coins. Once he caught his breath, Compton resumed rolling the barrel to the appointed site. There, his employer instructed him to pile wood around the keg. Upon completing the task, Compton was ordered to leave and never come again to the field. Reckoning that Kron was preparing to bury his treasure, Compton hurried back to his cabin as twilight descended on the mountains.

Several hours later, after darkness had engulfed the landscape, the distinct sound of chanting filtered into Compton's cabin. Hurrying to the doorway, he was startled to see a roaring fire in the field at the spot where he had left the keg. Around the inferno, several unrecognizable figures were performing some sort of ritualistic dance.

His curiosity aroused, Compton disobeyed Kron's prohibition and skulked over to the tree line at the edge of the field, some 150 feet from the bonfire. His hiding spot gave him a clear view of the strange activities taking place. Speaking and singing in an unfamiliar language and prancing around the blaze were Kron and two naked Indians. As the fire grew in intensity, the coins melted into a golden ooze. Meanwhile, the excitement of the dancers mounted, their unearthly shrieks piercing the quietness of the Uwharrie night.

Mortified by the spooky spectacle, Compton rushed back to his cabin, gathered up his meager effects, and left the area forever. Firm in the belief that Dr. Kron was a demon who might cause all manner of evil to befall him, Compton kept the story of the bizarre incident to himself until death came calling many years later.

What Dr. Kron was doing that autumn night remains a subject of speculation. Perhaps he intended to hide his treasure for his family's future use. Be that as it may, his daughters never found the melted mass of gold. Honoring their father's request, the girls did not marry, choosing instead to live the rest of their lives as spinsters on the plantation. But since they lacked the means to maintain the place, they were forced to sell various parcels of land over the years. When the second sister died in 1910, the final piece of the estate was liquidated to pay debts.

In the years that followed, the Kron homestead stood vacant in the Uwharrie wilderness. But throughout the area, there lingered rumors that gold, a large quantity of it, was hidden at the site.

One of the people most familiar with the tales of buried treasure was Birdsy Ponds, the nephew of Dan Compton. At length, Ponds decided to act upon the information provided by his uncle on his deathbed. Accompanied by two friends, the Sikes brothers, he called on a local conjure woman who lived at Feather Bed Hill. She confirmed that Kron had buried his gold where Uncle Dan had indicated. But she warned that the physician had also left behind lingering evil. He had summoned a horrifying force of spirits, witches, ghosts, haunts, boogers, demons, and minions to guard his land and to ward off treasure seekers.

According to the conjure woman, there was a way for the gold to be taken safely. She directed the men to go to the Kron place between dusk and midnight when the moon was full on the anniversary of the night the treasure was buried. Before digging, they were to follow a ritual: each man was to cross his heart, turn in the direction of the home, and call out, "Ye ghosts of the Kron gold, don't you bother me tonight." The conjure woman then had a surprise for the men: the gold had been buried on that very night many years ago. Unfortunately, they already had plans to attend a big dance. They reasoned that the treasure would wait for them one more night.

After the sun went down the following day, the three men arrived at the Kron place with lanterns in one hand and digging implements in the other. About them was the stillness unique to the Uwharries. Whether they performed the suggested ritual is unknown, but before they could turn a thimbleful of earth, ominous sounds descended from Mount Hathaway. Fearful that wild animals were about to stampede them, the threesome scrambled for the cover of their wagon. But as the terrible noise passed their position, there was nothing in sight.

Again the fellows made their way to the digging site, this time with a bit of extra caution. Once more, strange sounds emanated from atop the mountain, but now they resembled the thunder of hundreds of rolling wagons. To the relative safety of the wagon they fled. There, they waited until the phantom sounds ceased.

Despite their mounting fear, they returned yet again to the place where the gold was supposedly buried. Now, a popping sound prevented them from beginning their labors. Down the mountain came an appalling troop of cadavers and ghouls armed with cudgels, scythes, and similar weapons. These terrifying creatures emitted a strange, moon-like glow. Birdsy and the Sikes boys swung their tools wildly to defend themselves from the supernatural beings, but they were not attacked. Instead, the long line paraded to the digging site and vanished into the ground.

When the ordeal was over, the men collected their wits. Birdsy insisted that they had just witnessed the ghosts assigned by Kron to guard his gold. But the brothers considered it all a dream. They insisted that the search proceed, since the hour was hastening toward midnight.

With the first strike of a pick, the earth trembled with such force that all three men were thrown to the ground. One of the brothers, his anger now outweighing his fright, jumped to his feet and slammed his pick into the hole with all his might. It stuck so firmly in the ground that he could not extricate it no matter how hard he tried. He picked up a spade and obtained the same result. It was as if the implements were frozen in the ground.

The other brother stepped forward and, as if by magic, pulled both tools from the earth with little effort. But when he attempted to slam the pick into the hole, it bounced back as if it had hit solid rock. His frustration showing, he delivered a second powerful blow. This time, the pick penetrated the earth. And from the hole came an overpowering stench unlike anything the men had ever smelled before.

As they gagged and coughed, a heavy rain began to pour down upon them. Unable to escape the terrible odor, all three lapsed into unconsciousness. Birdsy came to first. He loaded the Sikes boys on to the wagon and drove them off the property.

Despite these unnerving events, the three men drove back over to the Kron place the next day. From their wagon, they could see that the hole was completely covered and that there was no sign of their recent presence. Never again did any of them look for the Kron gold for fear of incurring the wrath of the doctor's supernatural sentries.

As far as anyone knows, the gold remains buried in the Uwharries just where Kron put it. Visitors are welcome to tour his old homestead, but treasure hunting is strictly forbidden, since the property is owned by the state. And history would suggest that there is a far better reason to avoid the temptation to raid the hidden cache: the place is haunted by Kron's security force of ghosts and ghouls. Indeed, the doctor of the Uwharries left us with an enduring prescription for terror!

The Spirit of Independence

Nothing in life is to be feared. It is only to be understood.

Marie Curie

During the struggle for American independence, North Carolina had no greater Patriot than John Martin of Stokes County. Born in Albemarle County, Virginia, "Colonel Jack" Martin, as he came to be known, settled in western Stokes County as a young man in 1768. As differences grew between the colonies and Great Britain in the 1770s, Martin began the construction of a massive stone house in the shadow of Hanging Rock Mountain. Throughout the course of the war, the fortress-like structure served as a place of refuge for independence-minded neighbors seeking protection from marauding Indians and vindictive Tories. To this day, the ghost of one of Colonel Jack's neighbors is said to roam the remains of the ancient building.

From the war's beginning until its end, Martin rendered distinguished service as a Patriot officer. Just weeks after the colonies declared their independence in early July 1776, Martin marched with other troops from the area to take part in General Griffith Rutherford's campaign against the Cherokee Indians in the western Carolinas. As the war grew in intensity and scope, the young officer was conspicuous for his gallantry on numerous battlefields. But it was as a scout and guerrilla fighter that Martin achieved enduring fame.

Because his military duties kept him away from home for extended periods, Colonel Jack, then a bachelor, was unable to enjoy his architectural masterpiece during the war. Constructed of native stone, the towering, four-story structure resembled an English mansion from an earlier day. Its three-foot-thick outer walls were plastered with white stucco. On many occasions during the long fight, neighbors and friends living on the slopes and in the valleys of the Sauratown Mountains gathered at the Rock House, as it was known. They used the basement for a kitchen and dining room and the lower floor for living quarters. The upper floors served as a citadel from which the occupants could watch for and ward off attacks.

Because of his dedicated service to the cause of independence, Colonel Jack and his sturdy, imposing residence were favorite targets for the bands of Tories who operated out of the caves of nearby Hanging Rock. Hoping to find him at home, Loyalist raiders stormed the Rock House one day while Colonel Jack's neighbors were holed up there. During the melee, an unarmed woman was shot to death by the Tories as she stood on the doorstep of the stone dwelling.

After the war, Colonel Jack married and reared a family of ten children at the Rock House. For a number of years after America declared victory in 1783, the family endured harassment and reprisals by area Tories, who hated Colonel Jack for his spirited fight against the British Crown. Legend has it that some of the most vengeful of these men kidnapped a daughter of Martin's. Using a spyglass from a window of his house, Colonel Jack spotted a speck of color at Torys Den, a cave on Hanging Rock Mountain. It was his daughter, who was clever enough to wave her petticoat to attract attention. Her father promptly formed a posse, effected her rescue, and eliminated the last elements of Loyalist activity in western Stokes County.

Colonel Jack died at his plantation in 1822, but the estate remained in his family for an additional half-century. After the Rock House left the ownership of the Martins, local folks began to experience supernatural sights and sounds there. The ghost of the woman murdered in the doorway was observed moaning and groaning as she wandered about the structure. After that, few area residents were willing to venture near the Rock House after dark.

A devastating fire of unknown origin gutted the interior of the home in 1890. Ferocious storms in 1897 and 1924 claimed the roof and one of the exterior walls, thus rendering the house uninhabitable—for humans, at least. The ghost of the lady who sought refuge here while Colonel Jack was away at war continues to roam the premises. Eerie lights have been observed by persons who happened by the place at night. Even more disconcerting are the shuffling sounds and sharp noises coming from inside the shell of the structure. Passers-by who have heard the commotion have likened it to two bony hands being clapped together.

By the time the nation was preparing for its bicentennial celebration, the remnants of the Rock House were covered in vines and hastening to ruin. In 1975, the Stokes County Historical Society acquired the five-and-a-half-acre tract. Since that time, the site has been cleared and the tall walls stabilized.

Should you wish to visit this lasting monument to the stalwart Patriot who built it, the preserved site is located on SR 1187 (Rock House Road) ten miles from the entrance to Hanging Rock State Park. During the light of day, the rock walls are an awe-inspiring sight in a serene spot where blood was shed for the new American nation. At night, a ghostly guardian patrols the place. The fortress continues to be protected by the spirit of independence. Colonel Jack would have it no other way.

Phantom Patriots

If anyone tells you something strange about the world, something you have never heard before, do not laugh, but listen attentively.

Georges Duhamel

West of the Pee Dee River, there is a noticeable rise in elevation and change in soil composition. It is here that the Sandhills region of North Carolina gives way to the red clay of the Piedmont.

During the Revolutionary War, a perceptible difference existed in the loyalties of the people living east and west of the river. As in the Sandhills area, many of the Revolutionary War leaders of the southern Piedmont were Presbyterians. But on the west side of the Pee Dee, the Presbyterians were of Scots-Irish descent, and their loyalties were not to Great Britain. Rather, they were overwhelmingly supportive of the fight for independence.

A particular hotbed of patriotism was the Waxhaws, a region

that includes what is now Union County. A number of historic sites and markers in the southern half of the county call attention to the places and people that played a significant role in the Revolutionary War. But there are no signs calling attention to the invisible Patriot army that can still be heard rumbling down NC 200 south of Monroe.

One of the important local sites stands near the southeastern corner of the county at the South Carolina line, where monuments honor the man who symbolized the independent spirit of the people of the Waxhaws. Andrew Jackson was born here in 1766. Even though he was only nine years old when the colonies declared their independence, Jackson shouldered a musket for the American cause before the end of the war. A significant skirmish known as the Battle of the Waxhaws took place on September 20, 1780, just west of Jackson's birthplace on the plantation of Captain James Wauchope. Here, some 150 of Wauchope's comrades commanded by Colonel William R. Davie, a brash, young Carolinian, surprised and routed the right flank of the Redcoat army of Lord Charles Cornwallis. Fleeing the battlefield in utter confusion, the British soldiers set fire to the plantation house and outbuildings. They left behind 60 wounded soldiers, 20 of whom would die. Only a single Patriot soldier was wounded.

That isolated battlefield is quiet today. But seven miles up NC 200 near its intersection with SR 1146 (Parkwood School Road) at the community of Roughedge, ghostly sounds related to Revolutionary War combat in the area can often be heard.

One of the most ardent Patriots in southern Union County was Ned Richardson. He and his wife lived on a farm in the vicinity of Roughedge. During the war, Richardson was forced to spend much time away from his wife. Visits to his home were fraught with danger, for local Tories watched and waited for a chance to capture him.

Their opportunity came when Richardson's duties brought him to the site of what is now Monroe, the seat of Union County. His home was less than eight miles to the south, and his wife was expecting a child. Unable to overcome his desire to spend some time with her, he disregarded the peril and made his way to the farm. After his arrival, a band of sixteen Tories surrounded the cabin and informed Richardson that he was a prisoner. He was told that he could spend the night at the cabin, but that on the morrow he would be executed as a traitor to the British Crown.

In the dark of night, Richardson's wife escaped and rode to the Patriot camp, where she sounded the alarm to her husband's compatriots. Before the morning sun rose, a small army of Patriots had encircled the Tories and captured them. Ned Richardson emerged from his cabin and was afforded the "honor" of shooting the Loyalists. After he completed the executions, the corpses were dragged into the nearby woods and buried unceremoniously in unmarked graves.

Nothing remains of the Richardson farmstead of the eighteenth century. The tree near which the executions were carried out—long known as the Tory Tree—was removed in 1981 for road construction. But today, if you happen to travel through the Union County community of Roughedge on NC 200, don't be surprised if you experience an aural reminder of the Revolutionary War drama played out here. For as long as anyone can remember, the sounds of the galloping horses of the Patriot rescue party have been heard at this small settlement. Indeed, the spirits of American independence are alive and well in the Waxhaws.

Doppelgänger!

Everyone's different. The five fingers are not all the same.

Arabian proverb

On a certain evening in 1918, Scott Parker of Henderson, North Carolina, pushed the electric button at the door of the main entrance to a Baltimore hospital. When the doorman, a mature black gentleman, opened the door, he became highly agitated. His mouth dropped open, and his eyes filled with fear. Indeed, he looked as if he had seen a ghost. In a flash, he slammed the door in the face of the caller, and the bewildered Parker heard the sound of shoes pounding the interior hallway, as if someone were fleeing in terror.

What frightened the Baltimore doorman that night was not a ghost. Rather, it was a Doppelgänger. A German word, *Doppelgänger* is translated as "double walker" or "co-walker." It is most commonly used in the world of the supernatural to describe a ghostly double of a living person. Most often, the apparitional Doppelgänger cannot be seen by its human double. It is considered an omen of bad luck or a portent of death.

The Doppelgänger surfaced as a theme in several pieces of classic literature of the macabre. Mary Shelley employed the motif in *Frankenstein*, as did Robert Louis Stevenson in *Dr. Jekyll and Mr. Hyde*.

In the real world, some hold the belief that every person has a twin—identical in looks, physical characteristics, personality, and behavior—somewhere in the world. The chances of meeting your flesh-and-blood Doppelgänger are extremely remote. It is said that if you happen to encounter your real-life double, supernatural forces are at work.

There are some well-documented accounts of these rare meetings. One of the most incredible cases involved two men who were neighbors and best friends in the Vance County town of Henderson during the late nineteenth and early twentieth centuries. It was the unbelievable likeness between Scott Parker and John Missilier that so unnerved the Baltimore hospital attendant. But that part of the story is best left to the end.

As far as they or anyone else knew, Parker and Missilier were not related by blood. They were virtually the same age, and both were native North Carolinians. Parker was born in Wilson, and Missilier came into the world at New Bern. They were thirty years of age before they first encountered each other when they almost simultaneously and by happenstance moved to Henderson.

Parker was a man of small stature. He had blue eyes and weighed but 125 pounds, and he sported a mustache, sideburns, and cross-cut whiskers. His soft voice matched his kind, gentle personality. That description also applied to Missilier, for the two men appeared to have been poured from the same mold. On May 23, 1926, the *Raleigh News and Observer* ran pictures of the two men side by side. The resemblance between the two was uncanny.

Soon after they met, the two became the best of friends and soul mates. Transcending their exact likeness in physical appearance and personality were their common tastes and values. Parker and Missilier quickly came to the realization that they could not live in comfort or satisfaction without being in each other's immediate presence.

Life was not without difficulties for the nonrelated twins. They were often mistaken for each other on the streets of downtown Henderson, for if a person had ever seen Scott Parker, he had also seen John Missilier. Such was the confusion that it carried over to family members. On one occasion, Parker's two-year-old granddaughter saw Missilier on the street and promptly ran to the man she thought to be her grandfather. Missilier carried the child in his arms to the Croatan Club, where he knew Scott Parker to be. When the little girl saw the two men together, she could not ascertain which was her grandfather.

As to this strange case of sameness, Parker took the matter very seriously. He looked upon it as a mere coincidence, an inexplicable freak of nature. On the other hand, the more upbeat Missilier saw it as a humorous joke played on the men. To that end, he always relished the opportunity to make light of the unbelievable likeness.

One day, Parker found Missilier at the club and greeted him thus: "I've been hunting for you. What have you been up to now?"

With a twinkle in his eye, Missilier replied, "Oh, nothing much. Say, Scott, do you know a man named Dinkins over near the Franklin line?"

Parker nodded. "Bill Dinkins. He ran up an account with me for about five hundred dollars and has never paid me a cent. What about him?"

"Well, I saw him on the street today, and he mistook me for you."

"What did he have to say?" Parker asked.

With great delight, Missilier explained, "Oh, nothing much. Our conversation was very brief, and he left rather hurriedly. But he did seem to be very grateful."

"Grateful for what?"

"Why, Dinkins came up and said, 'How do you do, Mr. Parker? You're the very man I'm hunting for. Mr. Parker, I sold that old field piece of mine, and I cleaned up. I've come to settle that old account of mine, and to pay interest, too. If you would figure it out, I will write you a check right now.' "

Parker was now hanging on every word, so Missilier quickly delivered the clincher: "I said, 'Why, Dinkins, old fellow, I'm delighted to hear of your good luck. But you need the money more than I do. As to that old account, why, I'd almost forgotten it. Keep your money, man.' "

Parker was not amused, but neither could he get terribly angry with his beloved Doppelgänger. Nevertheless, the prank caused Parker to suggest that they should change their appearance so people could distinguish them. When Missilier would have none of it, Scott took matters into his own hands by shaving off his mustache. Rather than be different, Missilier followed suit.

Missilier's mischief continued. Parker owned a farm pond in a secluded area of the Vance County countryside. A tall barbed-wire fence surrounded the pond, and the gate was locked tight at all times. When he arrived at the pond after a two-week vacation, Parker was informed by his farm tenant that a moonshine still was in full operation on the fence-enclosed pond. Because of the threatening nature and appearance of the three men running the still, the tenant had refused to intervene.

Parker immediately armed himself with a shotgun and supplied one to the tenant. As the two men made their way toward the pond, they were accosted by several heavily armed revenue officers. Recognizing the property owner, one of the officers said,

"This looks bad for you, Mr. Parker. One of the men we are guarding over there says he put up the still with your full knowledge and consent and that you urged him to make a quick run."

The prisoner in question chimed in, "Oh, yes, he can't deny it. He's in it, too. He urged me to go ahead, said he wanted some liquor hisself, and the bargain was he was to get half of the first run. Now, didn't you, Mr. Parker? I saw you last Sadday. You know I did." But this time, it was Scott Parker who was determined to have the last laugh on his Doppelgänger. Very firmly, he said to the officer, "See here, Tom. Look behind my right ear. Do you see anything?"

After doing as he was instructed, the officer responded, "Nothing but three long gray hairs."

A look of satisfaction on his face, Scott said, "Well, you find John Missilier and look behind his right ear, and see if you don't find a black mole. This man is right in supposing that I agreed to let him put up his still here, but I can prove by more than twenty witnesses that I was three miles off Shackleford Banks fishing last Saturday, that I have been away for two weeks and returned last night. See Missilier and examine his right ear."

For thirty years, the jokes, tricks, and merriment continued unabated. Rather than existing as if they had been sentenced to a lifetime of sameness, Scott Parker and John Missilier enjoyed happy lives filled with the wonder and enchantment of their oneness.

The end of this tale brings us to its beginning. After having the hospital door rudely slammed in his face, Scott Parker was greeted by an intern and two nurses wearing perplexed looks on their faces. After closely scrutinizing the visitor, they invited him inside and ushered him to a room. There, they closed the door and once again eyeballed him from head to toe.

Breaking the growing tension, the intern offered an apology: "Of course, you will excuse us, sir, but as you were not here when he died, we didn't know he had a twin brother."

Parker inquired, "Who had a twin brother?"

And then came the response Parker feared: "Why, Mr. Missilier, of course, for you are either Missilier's twin brother or Missilier himself. And you cannot be Missilier, for he died yesterday on the operating table."

Doppelgänger!

Capitol Haunts

A footstep, a low throbbing in the walls,
A noise of falling weights that never fell,
Weird whispers, bells that rang without a hand,
Door handles turn'd when none was at the door,
And bolted doors that opened of themselves . . .

Alfred, Lord Tennyson

Raleigh, selected in 1792 as the "inalterable capital of North Carolina," is truly a haunted seat of state government. The Executive Mansion, the home of every governor since 1891, is inhabited by the ghost of its very first resident, Governor Daniel Fowle. Almost within the shadow of the governor's residence stands the historic North Carolina State Capitol, which houses the offices of the governor. Roaming the rotunda, the staircases, and the chambers of this imposing edifice are ghosts of unknown origin.

Since its completion in 1840, the Capitol has graced the center of downtown Raleigh at Union Square. From 1840 until 1963, when the State Legislative Building—the first building constructed in the United States for the sole purpose of housing a state legislature—opened, the North Carolina General Assembly conducted its sessions in the Capitol. During that long period, many of the most famous Tar Heel statesmen wrote the state's political history through their debates and decisions. Today, the magnificently preserved Greek Revival structure, one of the smallest of the nation's state capitols and a National Historic Landmark, plays host to infrequent ceremonial sessions of the legislature. Each year, more than two hundred thousand people, many of them schoolchildren, visit this grande dame of North Carolina government to tour the authentically restored legislative chambers and the former state library. But few, if any, of the tourists are around when the Capitol ghosts make their nocturnal appearance.

Capitol employees have experienced the mysterious things that take place here after the sturdy building is locked for the evening. Take Owen Jackson, for example. Jackson, a tall, white-haired security guard who worked nights in the building for more than fifteen years in the last quarter of the twentieth century, had more encounters with the Capitol phantoms than he could count.

On more than one night, the trusted guard scrambled upstairs upon hearing the sound of books falling in the re-created former state library on the third floor. But upon his arrival, no books were ever missing from the shelves. One evening in 1981, Jackson heard the distinct sound of a breaking window on one of the upper floors. After he secured a broom to clean up the expected mess, he found no broken glass anywhere, despite a thorough search.

On his nightly rounds, the guard would sometimes detect the movement of the ancient elevator, which was operated manually from the interior of the car. From floor to floor the elevator would move, its doors opening as if to allow a phantom to get off.

One night in 1982, while at his station at the reception desk on the first floor, Jackson heard the unmistakable sound of footsteps on the staircase behind him. He later provided the details of the frightening incident: "They went step . . . step . . . step. It sounded like they were old and arthritic, they were moving so slow, taking one step at a time. But I didn't see a thing."

An often-discounted legend about the building is that the steps of the west staircase on the interior were damaged when whiskey barrels were rolled up and down them in the distant past. Nevertheless, on one occasion, Jackson heard what appeared to be a barrel being slowly rolled down the steps.

One dark evening in early 1984, the roar of a violent wind attracted his attention. It lasted only sixty seconds or so, but according to Jackson, it "sounded like it was blowing inside and outside." He scurried over to the window, where he fully expected to witness the tops of the tall oaks on the grounds swaying. What he saw—or, rather, did not see—startled him: "There weren't a leaf moving or a branch moving anywhere. After a minute, it stopped. Got just as quiet. If you'd been stone deaf, it couldn't have got no quieter. I know it was a haint."

The acoustics in the cavernous building are outstanding. Sounds echo off the thick stone walls, enabling them to be heard throughout. As Jackson put it, "A little fuss goes a long way in here."

He heard his most terrifying "fuss" about an hour before midnight one stormy evening, when the bloodcurdling scream of a woman resonated from the second floor. From his position at the reception desk, Jackson thought to himself, "It sounds like someone got her." But the guard did not move because, as he explained, "If she really needs me, she'll scream again."

Jackson also experienced the touch of a Capitol haunt. He

was sitting at the reception desk just before the start of his rounds when it happened: "I felt someone's hand on my shoulder. I could tell it was a hand because I could feel the weight of it, but when I turned around, there was no one there."

Other Capitol staff members have experienced similar sensations. As curator of the building, Raymond Beck was aware of Owen Jackson's alleged brushes with the supernatural, but he dismissed them as mere fancy until a spring night in 1981. On that evening, Beck worked late in the old state library. As he stood up to reshelve some books, an odd feeling came over him: "I felt as though someone were standing behind me looking over my shoulder—the same feeling you get when you're seated at your desk and you can sense that someone has come up behind you. That happened twice, and I didn't give it a third chance, because I closed up shop and went home."

Later that year, Beck mentioned his unusual experience to Sam P. Townsend, Sr., a man who retired at the close of the twentieth century after a long and distinguished career as administrator of the Capitol. To Beck's surprise, Townsend admitted that a similar thing had happened to him in the same room.

Townsend, an engineer by training, is a pragmatic man who sought to find scientific explanations for the bizarre things that he observed in the building. He once noted, "I work a lot at night. I'm careful not to give supernatural explanations for the noises, because they can't be proven. Our department is based on historical research."

But there were things he experienced in the Capitol that he could not readily explain. About eight o'clock on a June evening in 1976, Townsend was putting the finishing touches on the paperwork necessary for the reopening of the newly restored building. At the time, he was working in the governor's office, located near the south entrance. When keys began to rattle in the lock of the door at the north entrance, Townsend supposed that

Thad Eure, the longtime secretary of state, was returning to his first-floor office, as was his custom many nights. After the big door opened, Townsend walked out of the governor's office and across the rotunda to greet Eure. But Eure was not in the building. Suddenly, keys began rattling in the door at the south entrance, but that door did not open. A thorough search of the building and its grounds offered no clues for the mysterious occurrences.

Less than a year later, Townsend had another encounter with the Capitol haunts. His office was located on the second floor in the room formerly occupied by the clerk of the Senate, located at the northeast corner of the Senate chamber. While hard at work at his desk one night in 1977, he heard approaching footsteps that seemed to be coming from the direction of the former committee room on the northwest corner of the chamber. Expecting to see Raymond Beck when he opened the door, Townsend found no one. Over the next several years, he heard the same phantom footsteps at the same time each night—about eight-thirty. They stopped when a copy machine was placed in the room.

Sam Townsend not only heard the sounds of the building's ghosts and sensed their presence, but also caught a glimpse of them on several occasions. As he headed toward the Senate chamber en route to his office one evening, he was startled to see someone standing inside the doorway. In an instant, the phantom figure was gone. On another night, a dark gray form floated past Townsend in the rotunda, forcing him to take evasive action. "I swerved to avoid a collision," he later said.

Owen Jackson also caught sight of a ghostly presence in the building. Upon completing his duties one midnight, he turned off the lights—save those for security—checked all the doors of the empty building, and made his way to his automobile. While waiting for the vehicle to warm up that cold night, Jackson looked up and saw a figure walking past an illuminated window on the second floor: "The shade was pulled down halfway, but I could see a man that had a Confederate soldier's uniform. You could see the brass buttons shining on his jacket." Jackson shook his head in disbelief and promptly sped away. When asked why he did not reenter the building and confront the thing he had seen, the watchman quipped, "I figured anybody been dead that long, I didn't want to tangle with him."

Despite the many strange and unexplained incidents that occurred during his career at the Capitol, Owen Jackson never lost his sense of humor about the ghostly goings-on. Many times on his way out of the building after an eerie night of work, he would pass the exquisite copy of Antonio Canova's statue of George Washington, located in the rotunda. Cognizant that no watchman would replace him after midnight, Jackson would smile at the masterpiece and say, "Let George do it!"

But Owen Jackson was also serious about the bizarre things he experienced here. When asked about his frequent encounters with the supernatural, he commented with a shudder, "They don't make you feel good, but they won't hurt you." When challenged about what he had heard and seen, Jackson was adamant: "I'm a Baptist. I don't lie."

Raymond Beck also supposed that some of the strange occurrences might be of supernatural origin. "Maybe you can attribute some of these noises to the settling of the building and the heat and expansion of the roof," he said. "But when you think of the people who have been here since the 1840s—the governors, the Union troops—you have to wonder if there aren't lingering presences."

Sam Townsend, perhaps the most skeptical of the three men, readily admitted that he had no satisfactory explanation for the unusual sights and sounds.

No one knows the identity of the phantoms that haunt the

Capitol. Maybe some of them are the spirits of Democrats and Republicans who did political battle in these hallowed halls. Or, given Owen Jackson's sighting of a spectral Confederate soldier, perhaps one of the ghosts is that of a Southern warrior maintaining a lonely vigil over the Capitol. For, you see, it was in this building that it was decided on May 20, 1861, that North Carolina would secede from the Union and join the Confederacy. And almost four years later, following the fall of Richmond and Lee's surrender at Appomattox, Raleigh was the last significant state capital under Confederate control; Union troops finally occupied the mostly evacuated city on April 12, 1865. The speculation is endless.

Daylight tours of the fascinating building are available. History abounds in every nook and cranny. And so do ghosts. Don't expect to see one, however, for it seems that they come out to play only after the doors are closed to the public. These Capitol phantoms no doubt represent unknown North Carolinians of the past. For that reason, we perhaps shouldn't question their presence, because, after all, this haunted place is "the People's House."

WARREN COUNTY

The Devil's Footprint

The devil's best ruse is to persuade us that he does not exist.

Charles Baudelaire

Throughout history, many people have claimed that they have seen the devil in North Carolina. Their eyewitness descriptions of the Prince of Darkness have varied considerably. That is not surprising, because it is believed that he has the ability to appear in any form and size imaginable by humans. To deceive, Satan can take the shape of a man, woman, or animal. And to strike fear in his victims, he can manifest himself as a monster.

There is a far greater number of North Carolinians who, although they have not seen the devil personally, know of a place where he is said to have walked the Tar Heel landscape. Some of the most famous of these are the site of the mysterious hoof prints at Bath and the Devil's Tramping Ground in Chatham

County. A lesser-known site in Warren County is known as the Devil's Rock. The devil may have left a lasting impression here during one of his visits to North Carolina.

Located in a pasture off SR 1131 in the small Warren County community of Largo, the Devil's Rock measures about thirty feet long and fifteen feet wide. It is an enormous flat area of solid stone that projects just far enough above the surface of the ground to remain free from a soil covering. At one time, this unusual outcrop—which is the exposed portion of an extensive underground vein—was much larger. Significant portions of it were blasted away in the twentieth century for road construction. But neither man nor nature has been able to eradicate or alter the strange imprints in the rock.

Almost in the exact center of the Devil's Rock is a footprint twelve inches long and one inch deep. Imprinted in the stone several feet away are numerous tiny tracks, some of which overlap each other. They give the appearance that little children once danced upon the rock. Nearby is another indentation. This circular sunken area is the size of a snare drum. When tapped with a rock or stick, it makes a hollow sound.

No one knows exactly how long the mysterious impressions have been here. But it has been shown that early Warren County residents noticed them and speculated as to their origin. For as long as anyone can remember, folks in these parts have believed that the largest imprint in the stone is the right footprint of the devil, who is said to have walked here at night. On his visits, he beat his rock drumhead as his children danced in mirth and mischief. Those who intruded on these nightly rituals were severely punished. There are stained portions of the rock that appear to have had liquid spilled or splattered on them. Could this be the blood of visitors who unwittingly came to the rock when the Prince of Darkness was in residence?

As early as the antebellum period, area residents observed a strange phenomenon about the rock. Children at play while the sun was bright enjoyed filling the stone footprint with pebbles. Invariably, when they returned the next day, the pebbles were gone and the print was empty.

You may be wondering what happened to the left footprint of the devil. An evangelist who came to Largo to hold a series of religious services in the middle of the twentieth century examined the right footprint at the Devil's Rock. He informed the local citizens that he had once seen an identical left footprint in stone in South Carolina!

Skeptics scoff at the notion that this strange rock in rural northeastern North Carolina is one of the favorite haunts of Satan. But who among them has been willing to venture forth on a dark, brooding night to observe what goes on at the place called the Devil's Rock?

The Roots of America's Most Famous Haunting

*There is an evil spirit, who is extremely powerful and in-
telligent, and does his utmost to deceive me.*

René Descartes

The story of the Bell Witch is regarded by many
as the most frightening in American history, and the old John
Bell farm in Adams, Tennessee—the site of many of the terrifying deeds of the legendary witch—is ranked consistently as the
most haunted place in the United States. Few people realize,
however, that the principal players in the macabre drama were
native Tar Heels who first came in contact with each other in
the Town Creek area of northern Wilson County in the latter
part of the eighteenth century. Moreover, the evil spirit that was
the Bell Witch maintained close contact with and even visited
North Carolina while the drama was being played out.

John Bell, the principal target of the Bell Witch, was born in
Halifax County, North Carolina, in 1750 to a successful farmer

and respected citizen. Well educated for his time, John grew up in the Tarboro area and prospered at an early age as a cooper. In 1782, he married Lucy Williams, the daughter of John Williams, a prominent and wealthy resident of Edgecombe County. (At that time, what is now Wilson County was yet a part of Edgecombe.) Soon after their marriage, the newlyweds purchased and settled on land southwest of the several northern prongs of Town Creek in upper Wilson County near the community of Rosebud. For the next twenty-two years, the Bells lived there and reared a family of six children.

Among their neighbors for a time in the Town Creek area were Frederick Batts and his wife, Kate. A corpulent woman of more than two hundred pounds, Kate Batts was the eccentric who gained notoriety as the Bell Witch. Contemporary accounts of her as "pretty as sin" and "kindly as the Devil" were rather unflattering on the subjects of her physical appearance and demeanor.

By 1804, John and Lucy Bell reckoned that their family and slaves had outgrown the farmstead in Wilson County, so they looked west. That same year, they joined others—including the Batts family—in forming a wagon train that made its way across the mountains into Tennessee. There, the Bells settled on a site selected by John. Located fifty miles north of Nashville in Robertson County, the thousand-acre tract consisted of fertile bottom land along the Red River. John Bell constructed a spacious one-and-a-half-story log cabin for his family, along with numerous outbuildings.

Had John Bell known that Kate Batts would settle on land adjacent to his plantation and that she would bring with her the evil that would terrify his entire family and ultimately claim his life, he most likely would have remained in North Carolina. Nonetheless, for thirteen years, John and his family lived a happy life in their new home. His plantation proved quite profitable, and his wife gave birth to three more children. Because of his piety and his work ethic, John won the admiration and respect of his neighbors, save one—Kate Batts.

"Old Kate," as she was known in the community, assumed control of her family's property in Tennessee after her husband, a hopeless cripple, could no longer manage their business affairs. In her business dealings with local men, Kate was characterized as overbearing, obstinate, and unyielding. Her venomous tongue showered profane epithets on the men who fell into her disfavor. Extremely distrustful of her neighbors, the woman was convinced that everyone was out to cheat her.

It was little wonder, then, that Old Kate had a squabble with neighbor and fellow North Carolinian John Bell. She accused him of fraud after he purchased a tract of land from her to round out his holdings. En route from Red River Baptist Church to her home on a day soon after the transaction, Kate was heard to exclaim as she passed the Bell home, "Oh, yes, old John Bell, you have your broad acres and your comfortable home, and the future may look bright to you, but just wait and see what sad changes are soon coming to you and a certain member of your family."

John discounted the threat as the ramblings of a quarrelsome and rather queer neighbor. But he should have paid heed to it in light of the commonly held belief among local women that Old Kate was a witch. Their fears were well founded. On one occasion, a neighboring housewife spent considerable time and energy at the churn, only to produce no butter. In a fit of rage, she plunged a red-hot poker into the milk-filled churn and exclaimed to a friend, "I verily believe old Kate Batts has bewitched this milk, and I'm going to burn her out." Then the lady charged across the field to the Batts homestead to confront Kate. She found her suffering extreme pain, having badly burned her hand with a poker just moments earlier.

Kate subsequently accused John Bell of usury in a slave deal and requested that their church investigate the matter. Following an acquittal by the religious body, she lodged charges against him in the state court of Tennessee. In August 1817, Old Kate prevailed upon a Robertson County jury to convict her neighbor. That trial led to his expulsion from the church.

The evil force that would kill John in 1820 first made its presence known to members of the Bell family after the court proceedings concluded. One day, John and his twenty-one-year-old son, Drewery, were walking through a cornfield when they encountered an animal with the body of a dog and the head of a rabbit. John attempted to shoot it, but the strange creature vanished. Neither of the men thought any more about the unusual occurrence until the family heard an eerie beating sound on the outside walls of the house. Then a frightening mixture of noises filled the interior: knocking on doors and windows; scratching inside the walls; wings flapping against the roof; and the crying and growling of fighting animals. Night after night, the disconcerting sounds grew in intensity. John and his two adult sons searched every nook and cranny of the cabin for burrowing or nesting creatures but found nothing. In an attempt to allay the fear that was gripping his wife and children, John attributed the incidents to earthquake activity or vandals.

But then came nocturnal disturbances that could only be supernatural activity. Covers were mysteriously pulled off beds throughout the cabin. Chilling sounds filled the bedrooms: gulping, choking, strangling, smacking lips, a constant gnawing on the bedposts. Sleep became a rare occurrence in the Bell household.

Before a year passed, the haunting turned violent. Family members would be slapped about the face with such force that the hand print of the invisible assailant could be seen for a week. Their hair was frequently pulled at night.

John and his youngest daughter, Betsy, were subjected to the most severe physical abuse. Betsy, eleven years old, fell prey to fainting spells, followed by smothering episodes. Years later, the spirit broke up her engagement to be married. Poor John developed an unusual illness that afflicted his tongue and jaw muscles and made it difficult for him to chew and swallow. At his wit's end, he revealed the terrible plight of his family to a close friend, James Johnson, and asked for his help. Johnson agreed to stay in the house to experience the haunting. After his bed coverings were violently ripped away in the middle of the night, Johnson asked the spirit to identify itself. No answer was forthcoming.

But in the days to come, the witch indeed spoke. First, it claimed to be the spirit of an Indian buried in the nearby woods. Then it claimed to be the spirit of little Benjamin Bell, John's fourth son, who had died and was buried in North Carolina in 1798, before his first birthday. Finally, the spirit announced, "I am nothing more or less than Old Kate Batts's witch, and I'm determined to haunt and torment Jack Bell as long as he lives." Everyone present heard the witch when she proclaimed that she would kill John. And in time, she did.

After the witch began speaking, she did not cease. She recited, verbatim, sermons and prayers offered in the local churches, as well as private conversations between married couples in their bedrooms.

The locals made various efforts—ranging from exorcism to physical force by the area's strongest men—to rid the Bell home of its witch. As news of the haunting spread, people came from great distances to see the witch throw dishes and furniture and make wild pronouncements. John Bell welcomed all visitors with generous hospitality.

On the morning of December 20, 1820, the Bell Witch made good on her promise to kill John Bell, poisoning him by replacing his medicine with a brown, toxic substance. At John's bedside, a dear friend cried out in anguish, "The damned witch did this."

Instantly, a horrifying voice replied with glee, "He will never get up. I did it."

While she haunted the Bell family, Old Kate made numerous visits back to Wilson County. She provided John's wife, Lucy—a family member Kate actually liked—accurate details of what was going on with Mrs. Bell's family in eastern North Carolina.

There were other ways in which the Bell Witch exercised her powers in the Tar Heel State. John Bell, Jr., the second oldest of the Bell children, was the only family member who regularly assailed the spirit for the evil she visited upon his kinfolk. As a result, Old Kate maintained a healthy respect for him. She once informed John Jr., "You may not understand all I say to you, but remember, John, it will be true. Lies I have told to others were only to prove how foolish the average human really is."

True to her word, the Bell Witch used her supernatural knowledge in a futile attempt to spare John Jr. a fruitless trip to Wilson County and to provide him an opportunity to meet a potential mate. When the young man announced to the family that he was planning a trip to North Carolina to settle his father's share of an estate, Old Kate spoke up to inform him that he would come back empty-handed and that the long journey to Wilson County would be a waste of time. He was adamant about his plans even after the witch foretold the arrival of a beautiful young heiress in Robertson County.

John Jr. made his way to North Carolina, where matters were just as Old Kate had said they would be. While he was there for six months, lovely Felicia Norfleet, an affluent lady from Gates County, North Carolina, visited the Tennessee community where the Bell family lived. During her stay, many eligible bachelors called upon her, but John Jr. was not there. Unhappy with all the potential suitors she met, she returned to North Carolina, where she married a physician who subsequently committed suicide.

Skeptics who discount the authenticity of the Bell Witch would do well to remember that one of the most famous of all North Carolinians had a personal encounter with the evil spirit. As young men, both John Bell, Jr., and his older brother, Jesse, fought as junior officers under General Andrew Jackson during the War of 1812. From his fellow native North Carolinians, Old Hickory learned of the haunting at their Tennessee homestead. Following the war but before he was elected president, Jackson decided to call on the spirit.

As the general's wagon approached the Bell home, it suddenly stopped. The driver was unable to make the horses move. After inspecting the wagon, Jackson exclaimed, "It is the witch!"

From out of nowhere came Old Kate's voice: "They can go now, general."

Jackson spent the night in the Bell home, where he witnessed the witch's antics. Years later, after he took office as president of the United States, he recalled his night with Old Kate: "I saw nothing, but I heard enough to convince me that I would rather fight the British than to deal with this torment they call the Bell Witch!" When the witch spoke to the Bell family in 1828, she announced her intention to go away for 107 years. Since 1935, numerous strange lights, ghostly apparitions, and phantom sounds have been seen and heard at the old Bell Plantation site and in a nearby cave where the children of John and Lucy played. Some visitors to the site have claimed that they heard Old Kate's voice. Others have suffered physical violence from an invisible force.

And what about the presence of the Bell Witch in her native state in modern times? A rather tongue-in-cheek newspaper article in the *Raleigh Times* in 1965 indicated that the planned Rocky

Mount-Wilson Airport would be constructed in the Town Creek area if the Bell Witch did not interfere. But perhaps the article expressed a valid concern. During John Bell's lifetime, Old Kate returned home from time to time and always knew what was happening in North Carolina while she was away. If her spirit is alive and well in Tennessee today, as many people claim, then we should expect her to call every once in a while in Wilson County—the place where her roots lie.

Haunts of a Tragic Past

Those that set in motion the forces of evil cannot always control them afterwards.

Charles W. Chesnutt

Not even the most talented, the most artistic Hollywood designer could envision a haunted mansion to rival the old Dalton-Hunt House, located in the small Yadkin County community of Huntsville. Long vacated by human occupants, the once-grand two-story antebellum mansion is gradually being claimed by the elements. In physical appearance, it has all the trappings of a classic haunted house. On the exterior, the paint has faded and peeled from the wooden siding, numerous windowpanes are broken, and the front porch and overhanging balcony are unstable. On the interior, spider webs are everywhere, dusty, dilapidated furniture remains as a silent reminder of the last human residents, plaster has fallen from the walls, and the basement is dark and spooky.

Nor could the most creative writer of fiction develop a horror-story plot filled with the tragedy, murder, and otherworldly drama that were played out in the Dalton-Hunt House from 1840 to 1935. Ghosts, horrifying screams, and phantom lights are the eerie manifestations of this true tale of the macabre observed at the house today.

Around 1840, Henry J. Gorman, a master craftsman, built the house on land owned by his mother-in-law, Sarah Bird Dalton. The home's brick-floored basement was a rarity at that time in this area. The first floor contained a grand foyer and four large rooms; each of the rooms was ornately decorated with intricate plaster ceiling carvings, the handiwork of Henry Gorman. The second story was of equal size, and above it was a huge attic.

It served as the home of Mrs. Dalton, Gorman, and his wife, Julia A. Dalton Gorman. By all accounts, Mrs. Dalton and the Gormans enjoyed an affluent and happy lifestyle. Festive parties, balls, and galas made the home an inviting place. But then a series of tragedies transformed it into a dwelling of sorrow, death, and horror.

Paul Gorman, born to Henry and Julia in 1854, died suddenly when he was only four years old. Henry soon followed him in death. Unable to cope with these great personal losses, Julia went insane. She ultimately committed suicide by throwing herself from the second-story balcony. She was impaled when she landed on a cow stake and died instantly. Even now, her ghost can be observed walking and crying on the upper balcony.

Unwilling to continue living in a house that had become haunted, Sarah Bird Dalton moved to Texas, where she died around 1880. The house in Huntsville was sold by her estate to Dr. Leander C. Hunt, whose family would write a second chapter in the tragedy now synonymous with the decaying mansion.

Dr. Hunt was a well-respected physician who served more than a decade on the Yadkin County Board of Commissioners during the last quarter of the nineteenth century. Some sources indicate that the village of Huntsville was named for him, but it seems more likely that this settlement near the historic shallows of the Yadkin River received its name from Charles Hunt, who obtained a charter for a town here in 1792.

In 1879, the forty-one-year-old Hunt married Mary "Molly" Martin, who was fifteen years his junior. Molly, the daughter of a prominent local family, was a schoolteacher. Soon after purchasing the home, the Hunts established a social agenda of lavish parties and horse races, much in the manner of the former occupants.

After three years of wedded bliss, the Hunts became the proud parents of a baby girl on September 6, 1882. They named her Daisy. As the years passed, she matured into a beautiful, talented teenager. Hunt died when Daisy was fourteen. Thereafter, her mother became very protective of the young woman. The rather haughty Molly refused to allow Daisy to interact with any of the neighbors, believing that they were not of the proper social standing.

Despite her mother's best efforts to shelter her, Daisy met and fell in love with a local boy, Will Kelly. By early February 1902, Molly's worst fears were realized: her nineteen-year-old daughter was six months with child and without a husband. On the evening of February 2, those fears led to an act of terror that would forever haunt the house and grounds.

Early that day, Will Kelly entrusted a note to Joe Kimbrough, a laborer at the Dalton-Hunt House. Kimbrough was directed to deliver the note to Daisy that afternoon, because Kelly planned to stop by the mansion for her response after dark.

A heavy snow was falling when Will Kelly appeared out of the black night at the Hunt place. His attention was drawn to the barn, where Kimbrough was feeding the animals. Standing nearby was Will Martin, Daisy's maternal uncle, who lived at the house. According to Kimbrough, Martin pulled a pistol, aimed it at Kelly, and fired. Daisy's wounded suitor tried to flee, but

Molly Hunt suddenly appeared and blocked his route of escape. Martin moved in and pulled the trigger again. Kelly fell into the snow. His assailant, anxious to complete his mission of death, stood over the critically injured man and pumped a bullet into his head. During the course of the execution, Daisy had made her way out of the house to see her lover lying in the snow, which was now colored crimson with his blood. Somehow, Kelly managed to stand up, stumble to his horse, and mount it after three attempts. He rode away, but his wounds soon proved fatal.

When the sheriff of Yadkin County learned that Kelly had been murdered, he ordered an official inquest by the coroner. As part of the subsequent autopsy, Kelly's head was sawed open to locate the deadly bullet. Following the criminal investigation, Will Martin was indicted for murder by a grand jury. He promptly took flight and was never brought to justice.

Though Molly Hunt never faced any charges, many residents of Huntsville were of the opinion that she was the mastermind of the homicide. No one ever learned what was in the note meant for Daisy's eyes. Speculation in the community was that it was intercepted by Molly, who was incensed when she read Kelly's proposal that he and Daisy elope. Unwilling to chance her daughter's answer, the evil woman decided to eliminate her perceived problem.

On April 21, 1902, Daisy gave birth to a son. She named him Jack. She never revealed the identity of his father, but everyone presumed it was Will Kelly.

As the locals put it, the unfortunate baby was "marked" at birth as a result of the gruesome scene his pregnant mother had witnessed. Whether Jack Hunt was a monster child or simply an infant who suffered from a rare genetic disease was a topic of debate among all the people who saw him. Apparently born without sweat or oil glands, little Jack had scaly skin that gave him a reptilian appearance. As he grew, his unusual condition did not improve. Instead, his itching and bleeding skin tormented him all his life.

Because of Jack's physical deformity, his mother and grandmother reportedly hid him in the basement and did not send him to school or allow him to be seen in public. In effect, the Dalton-Hunt House became a tomb, for Molly and Daisy sequestered themselves there and lived lives of complete seclusion.

After Daisy died of cancer on August 1, 1934, at the age of fifty-two, she was interred in the cemetery at Huntsville Baptist Church. So was her impoverished mother when she died on May 13, 1935, at the age of eighty-three. Ironically, the grave of Molly Hunt lies within two feet of the plot where Will Kelly was buried.

Jack Hunt, the reptile-like child, grew up to become a vile, wicked man. Among his more heinous crimes were arson and two murders. When he passed away at the age of seventy-two on December 2, 1972 (the very day on which his grandfather, Dr. Leander C. Hunt, had died seventy-six years earlier), he was living in a shack near the once-stately home.

After the Hunt family died off, several ghosts joined that of Julia Gorman.

To this day, the spectral shape of a woman can be observed standing by a window. Is it the apparition of the overly protective Molly Hunt, or is it the spirit of Daisy waiting for the return of her lover, Will Kelly? No one knows for sure.

From the basement of the deteriorating structure come horrid screams, no doubt the unearthly cries of the ghost of the strange child who was hidden away there for years.

When darkness falls on this eerie place, orbs—small, round, translucent lights—float about the grounds. Orbs are generally believed to be the spirit of a deceased person. Might they be the supernatural presence of the murdered Will Kelly returning for the long-awaited response from Daisy?

Unless the Dalton-Hunt House undergoes an extensive renovation soon, it will be beyond repair. If it succumbs to the elements, North Carolina will lose one of its most famous haunted houses. Even so, maybe the final chapter can then be written in the great tragedies that overwhelmed the two families who called this place home. And perhaps its ghosts can finally be put to rest.